Buried Leads

By Amanda M. Lee

Text copyright © 2013 Amanda M. Lee

One

I'm being stalked.

I didn't realize it at first, of course. It was just a mild irritation.

My stalker started with simple emails: *What are you doing? How is your day? Are you dating anyone?*

Then it progressed to Facebook. It was a new account, so when I got the "friend" request, I didn't even hesitate. I didn't think it would be a big deal. Boy, was I ever wrong.

The online stalking started small -- just a lot of "likes" on my posts. I have a feeling, though, that if my stalker had a choice those would have actually been "dislikes."

As a reporter, I don't ever post anything personal on Facebook. Just a lot of links to my stories, general discussions on the weather – and the occasional pointed thread about how lazy my co-workers are. You know, normal stuff.

Then it progressed. My stalker started nagging me. Nothing major, just minor things: *You dress like that for work? Don't you think you spend too much time playing video games? Isn't it time for a haircut?*

Then, things started to get uncomfortable. My stalker started telling my co-workers and friends what they should be doing as well: *Don't encourage her to be obnoxious. I can see why she's so unbalanced, you people are unbalanced, too. You all need to see if you can get a group rate on a shrink.*

The stalking then spread to my cell phone.

At first, it was just texts: *Hi, how are you? What are you doing? Don't you want to talk to me? Why won't you answer me? Why are you so ungrateful? I won't forget this, believe me.*

It wasn't that I was purposely ignoring the texts – no really. It was just that I was legitimately busy. Then, when I read them, I was glad I missed them.

Things only got progressively worse – especially when the requests for Skype and FaceTime started coming in on a daily basis. I won't do that with anyone, let alone my stalker. I cannot fathom sitting in a chair and holding up a cell phone and taping myself talking to someone. It's too surreal to even contemplate.

Why am I telling you this now? Because my phone is ringing, and Caller ID is identifying it as my stalker. I want a witness in case the police need to be called – or dental records eventually become necessary.

"What do you want?" I probably shouldn't be antagonizing from the onset, but I've seriously had it.

"What are you doing?"

"I'm working."

"You're always working."

"So it should come as no surprise that I'm working now, should it?"

"Don't take that tone with me!"

"I'm not taking a tone! What do you want?" I'm seriously considering changing my phone number – even if it means I'll be cut-off from the sources I've cultivated over the last few years. That's how dire things have become.

"I want to know if you're coming for dinner?"

"I don't know yet," I hedged. It's best not to antagonize crazy people.

"Avery Elizabeth Shaw! You had better not miss dinner. You blew me off last time, and I will not tolerate you doing it again!"

Uh-oh, the middle name had come out. This must be serious. "Fine. I will make . . . every effort to make it to dinner."

"On time."

"On time," I lied.

"If you're lying, I'll come to your work – and I'll dance. Everyone will think I'm a crazy person."

There it was: the inevitable threat that would always make me crumble. "For crying out loud, I said I would come, *mom*," I practically exploded.

The sound of my mother's long-suffering sigh on the other end of the phone was enough to make my stomach tumble. I was definitely in for the world's biggest guilt trip when I did finally make it to family dinner. I had only missed one in the last six months – but that was a capital offense in my family. You can get arrested. You can go to rehab. You can accidentally drive a car into the river. You can't miss family dinner, though.

I hung up – after a few more minutes of steadfast promises that my attendance at family dinner would actually happen – and seriously considered throwing my phone through a wall.

My name is Avery Shaw. I'm a local reporter in Macomb County, Michigan, and I'm seriously considering going into witness protection to hide from my mother. I don't know when she discovered technology – but it's going to be the death of me, I swear. It was fine when she was just playing *Plants vs. Zombies*: that didn't affect me. It's quite another, though, when her obsession starts interfering with mine. I haven't even had a chance to play *Lego: Lord of the Rings* yet – and I've had the game for two weeks. That's just unacceptable.

I've been a reporter at The Monitor – Macomb County's longest running newspaper – for the past few years. I cover the police beat and general reporting. It's basically crime, politics and ordinary features.

Lately, besides being on my mother's own personal shit list, I was also on my boss' shit list. Last month, one of my co-workers had died in the parking lot. In my zest to uncover the truth about her death, I had inadvertently become involved in a huge drug bust that resulted in a few dead bodies, my cousin going to rehab, my co-worker getting caught in a house explosion and the pawnshop owner I was intermittently crushing on being shot. That was after I accidentally hit him with my car, of course.

I had spent the last month with my nose pressed to the grindstone – well, for me anyway – and I'd made a concerted effort to be a solid and reliable employee. No one at work seemed to believe my new work ethic would stick, though. I found their disbelief hurtful – and understandable. I'm not great with follow through.

"Who was on the phone?"

I turned to see my editor, Fred Fish, standing behind me. It was casual Friday, so instead of wearing his usual suit he was wearing a tracksuit straight out of the 1980s. It made so much noise when he moved, I was surprised he managed to sneak up on me. The online stalking by my mom was seriously starting to derail me. My natural survival instincts were on the fritz.

"No one," I answered with false brightness. I was used to Fish being irritated with me, but the outright hostility he'd been regarding me with lately was starting to get uncomfortable. I can't remember the last time he was this angry with me. It was probably when I called in sick on Jobbie Nooner Friday and went to the big boat party instead of covering it for the paper. I was caught when I showed up in the background of a few of our photographer's photos.

"No one?" Fish was regarding me suspiciously. I could see the glint of disbelief in his blue eyes as he peered at me over the top of his reading glasses.

"Just my mom," I conceded. I didn't want him to think I was hiding anything from him — at least right now.

"Was it important?"

Just her usual crap. "No."

"Good," Fish supplied. "I have an assignment for you."

This was a step in the right direction. He was giving me an assignment in person. For the last month, my assignments had consisted of a series of uncomfortably terse emails — and a stack of obituaries waiting on my desk when I got in each day. Ironically, most of those assignments hadn't required me to leave the building. I had the distinct impression he didn't trust me. I have no idea why. Granted, the murder of Darby, one of our editorial assistants, had taken a dark turn. I wasn't responsible for that, though. Very little of what transpired could actually be blamed on me. Less than half, really.

"What do you have?" I projected as much fake enthusiasm as I could. I was determined to get out of Fish's doghouse – even if it meant being one of those bright, shiny people I can't stand.

Fish shook his head as he regarded me. I don't think I was fooling him. "There's a missing woman out in Romeo."

"Romeo? I don't want to go to Romeo." So much for getting out of the doghouse. I said it before I even realized what I was doing. I'm not a chronic complainer. What? I'm not. I just don't want to drive to Romeo. It takes like forty-five minutes – and it's far too rural for my taste. I avoid any place that isn't inundated with fast food chains and coffee houses.

"Well, you're going," Fish dismissed my complaints with his patented hand wave. In other words, don't even bother starting to bitch. It won't work.

I sighed internally. I'd better just suck it up. "What do we know about her?"

"She's a 32-year-old mother of two," Fish supplied. "She's been missing about a week."

"Why are we just hearing about this now?"

"There was some confusion about whether or not she was on a work trip or not," Fish answered flippantly.

"Who's holding the press conference?"

"The sheriff's department."

Shit.

"If they're not sure that foul play is involved, why is the sheriff's department involved?" I don't have a problem with the police in general – okay, I do – but I really didn't want to run into one law enforcement official in particular right now. It just so happened it was Macomb County Sheriff Jake Farrell, my ex-boyfriend. Jake hadn't spoken to me since the drug bust debacle – and I wasn't looking forward to our first meeting happening at a press conference.

"I don't know," Fish answered stiffly. I could tell he didn't want any of my particular brand of drama to infringe on his day. "I guess you'll find out when you get out there."

I can't wait.

Fish handed me the piece of paper he was holding in his hand and walked away. I scanned it briefly. It was a press release from the sheriff's department. There was very little information on it. Just the basics. If I wanted to make it to the press conference on time, I would have to leave now.

I reluctantly grabbed my purse – it was a vinyl *Star Wars* model I had stumbled on at Hot Topic the week before – and a notebook and pen. I might as well get this over with. If I was going to get back in Fish's good graces, I would have to do a good job on this story. Even that might not work, but I had to start somewhere. I'm really sick of typing up obits.

Two

The drive out to Romeo is long and tedious. The Monitor is located in Mount Clemens, the county seat of Macomb. It has easy access to I-94 and Gratiot Avenue. Sure, it's located in front of a sewer plant and next door to a white trash flea market – but it's also close to the Clinton River and good coffee.

Romeo, on the other hand, is located in the northern end of the county. There's no easy way to get there. Essentially, the freeway doesn't go there. To get there, you have to take several smaller side roads. The farther you drive, the less there is to look at – besides trees. I know some people like that, but I've seen enough horror movies that it freaks me out.

It was early fall, so there were a lot of fruit and vegetable stands erected near the road on North Avenue. The homes out this way are generally old farmhouses with large gardens and a lot of empty acreage. The homeowners like to peddle their garden wares – and quirky craft projects -- this time of year. I was actually considering stopping at one on my way back and picking up some fresh corn. Hey, just because I mock it doesn't mean I don't like to eat it.

I followed the directions on the press release, pulling into a windy subdivision off of 32 Mile Road. This is a rich area. The homes are all at least two stories – and many are modern colonials intermixed with older Victorians. It's a subdivision – but it's not a normal subdivision. It is much more visually appealing.

I didn't have to look too long before I found where the press conference was going to be held. It wasn't hard. I recognized the Channel 2 news van from several blocks away.

I parked behind the news van, making a mental note that they were the only television presence in attendance. I saw a reporter I recognized from one of the larger Detroit dailies milling about, and several representatives of smaller weeklies in the area. This wasn't a full-blown media event – at least not yet. The whole circus only comes out for murders and synthetic drug busts these days. We're a cynical and hardened bunch, what can I say?

I searched the area surreptitiously for Jake – all the while pretending I was looking through my purse for a pen. I was relieved when I saw one of his investigators – Tony Winters – instead. It's not that I don't want to see Jake; I just don't want to deal with him when there's a crowd around. To say that he wasn't happy with me after what went down last month would be an understatement. Even though we hadn't dated since high school, there were times when we slipped back into old rhythms. The fact that I had *accidentally* stolen a flash drive with important evidence on it from one of his crime scenes hadn't exactly endeared me to him. The old rhythm we were slipping into at this point was outright rage on his part and mild contrition on my part.

I made my way over to the gathered reporters, greeting the two from the weeklies and nodding to the Detroit reporter. I ignored the television reporter. In general, reporters segregate themselves into two groups: Television and print. The television reporters are all about flash – and promoting themselves. The print reporters are all about finding the truth and reporting it in the best possible way. What? That is totally true. It's not just perception, I swear.

Tony smiled at me when he saw me. I couldn't tell if he was genuinely happy to see me – or if he was just entertained by the stories that, I'm sure, were flying around the sheriff's department about me. I'm something of a local celebrity. Celebrity, disaster, they're both the same thing aren't they?

"Hey, Tony."

"Avery, how are you?"

"Good," I lied.

"That's good. We'll be getting started in a minute."

"No hurry." I can't afford to piss him off, too. Right now, I'm persona non grata at the sheriff's department. I can use all the backup I can get.

"You're Avery Shaw?" I turned to see that the Channel 2 reporter had approached me. I recognized her vaguely. I think her name was Ariel Cook. She was young, with perfectly coiffed hair and a stylishly pressed suit. I hated her on sight.

"I am," I said to her stiffly.

"The Avery Shaw that was in the middle of that drug bust last month?"

I saw Tony try to hide his smile. "I wasn't in the middle of it," I protested. "I just happened to be at the wrong place at the wrong time." That's the story of my life. In fact, it will probably be the title of my autobiography: *Avery Shaw: She Was At the Wrong Place at the Wrong Time*.

"I thought a body was found at your cousin's apartment?" The reporter looked confused. I was guessing that was her perpetual state. She was named after *The Little Mermaid,* what do you expect?

"She didn't kill anyone," I argued. Lexie, my cousin, had been caught up with some very bad people. They had been manufacturing meth. Lexie, a chronic pot smoker, had decided to go to rehab after a nitrous tank exploded in the hallway of her building and she was evicted. She was due to get out of rehab any day now.

"I didn't say she killed anyone," the reporter didn't seem dissuaded by my tone. She'd learn.

"You insinuated she did," I countered.

"I did not."

"You did, too."

Tony swiftly stepped between us. "We're going to start the press conference now," he said smoothly.

Ariel Cook smiled at him sweetly. "Thank you, officer," she cooed.

What a fake. I glanced down at her shoes. Payless, no doubt. I noticed she was looking at my new Converse Arkham Asylum high-tops with equal disdain. I have a weird thing for shoes — but only if they're cute and comfortable. I think you can tell a lot about someone from their shoes. I could tell that this woman spent a lot on suits and nothing on shoes. What a waste. Of course, she probably took one look at my shoes and thought I belonged in an asylum myself — preferably that creepy one Jessica Lange is presiding over on FX these days.

Tony stepped to the center of everyone and started talking. He laid out the facts. Sarah Frank was, by all accounts, a reliable wife and mother. She worked for an insurance firm in Detroit, while her husband, Brian Frank, had a small business at home. Last Friday, after an argument with her husband, Sarah had left the house in a hired car that was supposed to take her to the airport for a flight to the Bahamas. No one had seen her since.

"When was she reported missing?" I asked.

"Yesterday," Tony answered.

"Why so long?"

"The husband thought that she was still mad and that's why she didn't call from the Bahamas."

The husband totally did it. What? I'm not jumping to conclusions. That would be unprofessional, after all.

"What did her boss say?"

"He said that, when Sarah missed the flight, he just assumed she had something going on at home. She had told him that she might not be able to make the trip and he figured that something had come up at home that had prohibited her from making the trip this week."

"Didn't he think it was weird that she didn't call and tell him that herself?" If I'm fifteen minutes late, Fish blows a gasket. I can't imagine just blowing off a week of work.

"Apparently, she had a great deal of autonomy at work – so it wasn't an unusual thing," Tony answered simply.

"Are there any signs of a struggle in the house?"

Tony frowned as he regarded me. "This is just a missing persons case right now, Avery."

"I was just asking." That was a pretty snippy answer for a standard question.

"Brian Frank is going to be coming out in a minute to make a statement to all of you," Tony said. "I would hope you would treat him as a man who is terrified about his missing wife and not a suspect." Tony's gaze was fixed on me.

"Of course," Ariel Cook said. "We don't want to add on to the pain he is obviously feeling. This must be terrible for him."

I couldn't stop myself from rolling my eyes. I noticed the two female weekly reporters were being unusually silent. They probably had no idea what was going on, I figured. They were just happy to be here – and getting a paycheck. Weeklies are generally the learning ground for dailies and dabblers. The lifers are true journalists at heart – but they're rare.

The front door of the house opened and I saw a small man – 5'8" at best – exit. He was small in stature and, as he grew closer, I was surprised at just how nondescript he really was. He had mousy brown hair, which was cropped close to his head, and curled in weird places. His green eyes were bright and red-rimmed. He'd obviously been crying.

"Hi," he greeted everyone in a low voice. He seemed timid. He didn't look like a murderer. Of course, very few murderers actually looked like they were capable of the deed.

"Brian wants to make a statement," Tony stressed pointedly. "He'll answer a few questions, but let's try not to overload him, shall we?" Tony was looking directly at me again.

"My wife is a wonderful person," Brian Frank started. "She's a great wife and a great mother. I just want her back. . . " He broke off as he fought off tears, choking on his own wrenching sob. He was either a really good actor, or he was really struggling with this.

"Was it unusual for her not to call for a week?"

Tony shot me a glare, but Brian didn't seem to notice. "Yes. I thought she was still mad at me, though. I just thought we would talk about things when she got back. She never came back, though."

"What did you fight about?"

"Just normal stuff," Brian answered. "Married people argue. I didn't think it was a big argument. I just wanted her to take fewer business trips and spend more time at home. I missed her."

Ariel Cook clucked sympathetically. "I'm sure she understood that."

"Has there ever been any domestic violence in the house?"

Brian looked up at me in surprise. His eyes nearly bugged out of his head. Now that I mention it, his eyes always looked like they were straining in his sockets. It was kind of weird.

"We've been married for seven years," Brian answered. "I loved my wife. I love my wife. I would never hurt her. I would never lay a hand on her."

"I have to ask these questions," I said honestly. "People are going to be wondering. We want people to be on the lookout for your wife. To do that, we have to convince them that you didn't do anything to her and you're not wasting our time."

Brian swallowed hard, wiping a stray tear from his face. "I know. You have a job to do. I also know that I can't find my wife without help. What else do you want to know?"

The press conference went on for another fifteen minutes. Most of it was just a rehash of how much Brian loved his wife. How much his children – Carrie and Mike – needed their mother. "I'm desperate for my wife to come home."

After everyone had exhausted their supply of questions, Brian handed out a card with his cell phone number on it. "Call me any time," he said. "I need to keep my wife's name in the news."

The Channel 2 woman maneuvered Brian over to an isolated part of the yard to do a private interview at this point and the two weekly reporters were heading towards their cars to leave.

I looked down at the photograph of Sarah that had been handed out a few minutes before. A small woman, with curly brown hair and bright green eyes stared back at me. She had a warm smile, I thought.

"What do you really think?" I asked Tony.

He feigned surprised. "What do you mean?"

"Don't play coy," I admonished him. "What do you think? Is she dead? Did he kill her?"

"We have nothing that points to that," Tony said stiffly.

"It's not normal to call a press conference at the victim's home," I pointed out the obvious.

"We wanted Mr. Frank to be as comfortable as possible," Tony replied. He was hiding something. I couldn't figure out what, though. Did they actually suspect Brian Frank, or was this just a fishing expedition?

"What's Jake say about all of this?" I asked finally.

Tony fixed his dark eyes on me. "You'll have to ask him that."

That wasn't going to happen anytime soon. At least I hoped.

Three

After leaving the Frank house in Romeo, I took the same route back to Mount Clemens that I initially used to traverse to the boonies. I stopped at one of the roadside stands and bought fresh corn and Brussels sprouts – and chatted with the woman running the stand.

When she found out where I worked, she seemed unusually excited. "That sounds like a cool job."

That's what everyone says. Saying the job didn't have its moments would be a misnomer. It can be exciting. Sitting through city council and water board meetings, though, is the actual definition of boring. Still, you don't want to tell random people that. They think you're just being snarky. Of course, I idle at snarky.

"It's okay," I said noncommittally.

"Why are you out here?" The woman looked around conspiratorially. "Are you busting a meth ring – like I read about that woman doing a month ago?"

"No," I shook my head vehemently, praying silently that she wouldn't put two-and-two together. I had to head her off before she had the chance to think about it too much. "There's a woman missing in Romeo."

The woman looked surprised. "Really? Who?"

"Her name is Sarah Frank," I said. "She lives out in Romeo."

"Do you think she's dead?"

I shrugged. "She's just missing right now."

"I bet it's human trafficking."

Human trafficking? People will believe anything that they see on television. It's not like human trafficking isn't a real thing – it's just not an everyday practice in Macomb County.

"I don't think so," I said. "She might have just taken off, for all we know."

"Is she married?"

"Yes."

"Her husband probably killed her." The woman was matter-of-fact. I couldn't help but smile to myself at how quickly she had flipped her conjecture on what happened, though.

"We shouldn't jump to conclusions," I admonished her. What? Just because I was thinking the same thing, that didn't mean that I was going to put it in print.

The woman pursed her lips at me. I could tell she didn't like my advice.

"I mean, I would have bet that Elizabeth Smart's parents did something to her – and I would have been wrong," I offered. "The same with Jon Benet-Ramsey's family."

The woman actually nodded at my statement. "You're right," she said. "It's just usually the husband, more often than not."

She had a point.

I took my fresh corn and Brussels sprouts and went back to the office. I took the vegetables into the office with me. I doubted being left in a hot car would hurt them, but I wasn't taking any chances. There's nothing worse than the smell of rotten fruit and vegetables, though.

As I made my way to my desk, I saw my friend Marvin Potts holding court in the center aisle of cubicles. Marvin had only been back on the job two weeks. He had been injured when the house of the woman he had been seeing blew up about a month ago. He was still milking the injuries he had sustained in the incident for all they were worth. A consummate hypochondriac, I had worried about the day when Marvin would actually get a real ailment. I had been right to worry.

"I still have a slight ringing in my ears," he was telling the court reporter. "The doctor says it may never go away. Other people that have had this problem slowly go insane."

"You're already insane," I pointed out, dropping the bag of vegetables on my desk and regarding him seriously for a second. "That's going to be a pretty short trip for you, isn't it?"

Potts smiled when he saw me. I was glad he wasn't holding me responsible for the explosion. It really hadn't been my fault – no, honestly – he just has bleeding tragic taste in women.

"So, is that woman missing or dead?" The court reporter – Jim Tolliver -- asked the question. I figured he was doing it for professional reasons more than anything else. It's not like we didn't get along. In fact, he was one of the few people in the room that didn't make me want to deafen myself with Q-tips on a regular basis, but we didn't sit around and gossip like school girls every day either.

"I don't know," I admitted. "If I had to guess, she's probably dead. She doesn't seem like the type of person who would just take off and abandon her kids. Of course, if I had kids, I'd probably want to abandon them, too."

"Did the husband do it?" Marvin was shuffling from one foot to the other. He was usually a fidgety individual, but his constant motion was a little distracting.

"I don't know," I answered. "He seems broken up about it. He could be acting, though. He did wait a week to report her missing."

Marvin was still shifting back and forth. "What's the deal? Why are you so nervous?"

"I'm not nervous," he said.

"Then why are you doing that?"

"Doing what?"

"That shuffling thing."

"I'm just in a good mood. Can't I be in a good mood?"

"Sure," I said hesitantly. "I've known you long enough to know that something else is going on, though, and you're dying to tell me. You might as well just get it out of the way."

Marvin scowled at me. "You think you know everything."

"I do."

"You don't know anything."

"Fine." I pulled my chair out and made a move to sit at my desk. Once I started writing, I wasn't going to be in the mood to listen to whatever bit of gossip Marvin wanted to spill – and he knew that."

"I met someone," he blurted out.

Oh, great. Marvin's love interests were getting progressively worse. If they weren't married and trying to get him to do homosexual threesomes they were Oxy addicts that had their houses blown up in drug busts gone wrong. I was almost terrified to hear about this new woman. "Where did you meet her?"

"She's a bartender at the Roost."

The Roost was a dive bar in Warren that Marvin frequented on a regular basis. The waitresses were all young, and scantily clad. I had been there a few times with him. I hadn't seen a waitress over the age of twenty-five. Since Marvin was fifty, the age discrepancy was starting to get noticeable. He kept getting older – and his love interests kept staying the same age. Pretty soon he was going to be Hugh Hefner – without the mansion, magazine and money.

"Has she graduated from high school yet?"

"Don't be judgmental," Marvin admonished me. He hated when I picked on the women he was dating – and yet he kept telling me about them. I think he got a perverse thrill out of me bad-mouthing them – I have no idea why.

"So, have you had sex with her yet?"

Marvin gave me a withering look. "She's a lady," he scoffed. "She doesn't have sex on the first date."

"Have you had a date with her?" That surprised me. His dates usually ended up as drunken fondling sessions in the backseat of his Pontiac.

"No, but I've asked her out and she's agreed."

Well, that was actually progress. "Where are you taking her?"

"We're going dancing at the Boat Basin in the Shores," Marvin said proudly.

I grimaced. I had seen Marvin dance. He had the rhythm of a deaf octogenarian. A deaf white octogenarian at that. "Well, that will be fun." I didn't want to rain on his parade. Once she saw him dance, I figured it would be all over anyway.

"I think she could be the one," Marvin said dreamily.

"The one what?"

"The one I'll marry and settle down and have kids with."

I blew out a sigh. Marvin met "the one" every couple of months. Usually those relationships ended up with some sort of police involvement. Still, I wasn't in the mood to get in a full blown fight with him. "Well, I hope it works out for you."

"Me, too," Marvin said happily.

I was happy to see that the perpetual whiner down the aisle had heard Marvin's pronouncement and was now grilling him on his upcoming happily ever after. Kim Hawk was one of those people that had a life-changing drama every day – whether it was legitimate (like a family member getting in a horrific accident) or not (her son dropping the F-bomb on his teacher).

I took advantage of Marvin's preoccupation with Kim and started to write my story. It really wasn't all that difficult. There wasn't a lot of extemporaneous information – so it was a straight-forward mystery at this point. I took the extra time to look up how many people had gone missing in the county last year, padding the story so it was more in-depth than it probably had to be. I was still trying to get off Fish's shit list.

When I was done, I shipped the story to the news queue and got back up from my desk. Marvin had just finished extolling the virtues of his new lady love and was walking back down the aisle.

He stopped at my desk long enough to pick up the press release and peruse the photos of the missing woman. "She's pretty," he said.

"Yeah, she looks nice," I said.

Marvin read through the press release in its entirety. He's a newshound. He actually sleeps with a police scanner next to his bed. He loves crime and crime stories. I could tell he was hoping this would turn into something big. I had a feeling he wasn't going to be disappointed. Unfortunately, a white mother of means disappearing from a ritzy suburb had Nancy Grace written all over it.

"Her husband's name is Brian Frank?"

"Yeah." I had no idea where he was going with this.

"He did it," Marvin said firmly.

"How do you know that?" I totally agree, by the way.

"He has two first names."

Even for Marvin, that was some circular thinking. "What do you mean?"

"His name is Brian Frank. Never trust anyone with two first names. They're always crazy. That's a proven fact. Everyone knows it."

Well, you couldn't argue with that.

Four

After I finished my story, I stopped by Fish's desk to let him know that it had been filed. My desperation to ease his dislike of me was starting to get a little pathetic. I recognized it – and yet that just made me more determined to get off his list. I was much happier when he was mad at my co-workers. I'm selfish like that; I can admit it.

Fish read the story and said it was "fine." I knew it wasn't exactly going to win any awards, but a little gushing wouldn't have hurt.

Instead, I decided it was time to call it a day. I didn't want to say anything that would come back to haunt me. That's a usual occurrence for me. I know when to shut my mouth, but I don't have the ability in a lot of situations. I decided to just remove myself from temptation. I had to be downtown anyway. I had a bridal fitting.

I'm not the one getting married, mind you. My best friend Carly had been involved in the marriage preparations of the century for the past six months. That meant less time for me – and more time for general bitching. I missed just being able to laze around on the couch and badmouth people with her – but I had more time for video games and movies without her petulant pouting about "wasting my time." It was a trade off. Of course, my mom was making up the slack on Facebook. I had a feeling it was a conspiracy.

Anyway, as her maid of honor, I was due for my second fitting on my bridesmaid dress. Usually, this is something I would essentially lie, cheat and steal to get out of. Carly and I had been best friends since college, though, and I knew there was no getting out of this. She knew all my tricks, anyway. Plus, I was genuinely happy for her. I loved her fiancé, Kyle, like he was my own brother. He was a good guy – and she'd made a good choice.

The dress, though, was another story. It was a lilac sheath that had very little give. I don't like heels – unless they're on a pair of really cute boots – but I didn't think Carly would allow me to wear my new cowboy boots to her wedding. When Carly tried to sell me on the dress, she kept saying it was something I could wear for years. Brides always say that – and it's never true. The only place I could see wearing this dress again was in my nightmares.

Carly told me the only reason I didn't like the dress was because it wasn't fitted properly yet. "It's just a sample sheath," she admonished me. "You'll like it when they take it in."

I doubted that, but I knew that letting her know how much I hated the dress would only hurt her. And, despite all evidence to the contrary at times, I don't go out of my way to hurt people.

I drove to downtown Mount Clemens, casting a wary glance at the pawnshop on the corner. I hadn't seen the owner, Eliot Kane, in weeks – not since he'd been injured in an attempt to save Lexie and me from a crazed stripper with a gun. The ensuing explosion had put him in the hospital. Before the incident, we had been steadily dancing around one another and flirting. Since then? Nothing. I found that I actually missed him.

When I got out of my car, I made sure to walk past his store so he could see me if he was working. I was disappointed to see a young woman working behind the counter instead of Eliot.

The easy thing to do would be for me to call him. I never do things the easy way, though. I never have. Instead, I made my way to the bridal shop – called New Beginnings – and entered.

The minute I walked into the store I felt like I was being smothered by white taffeta and chiffon. Blech.

"Good, you're here."

I turned to see Carly standing in the middle of the store and tapping her foot impatiently. She didn't look happy to see me. I saw her glance at her watch and fix me with a hard glare. "And you're only ten minutes late. That must be some sort of record for you."

"I had to file a story," I protested lamely.

"You always have to file a story," she said, striding forward and fixing her hand on my elbow securely. "If I had to guess, it's more like you were still groveling for your boss to forgive you."

She knew me too well.

"I was not," I lied.

"And now you're lying."

I bit my lip. I hated it that she knew me so well. Instead, I decided to distract her with something shiny – or lilac, whatever. "So, where's the dress? I can't wait to try it on."

Carly regarded me with her cool green eyes for a second. "That was pretty good. Keep that up while she's here."

"While who is here?"

"The Wicked Witch of the Midwest," she whispered in my ear.

Oh, no. Carly's future mother-in-law was here. The woman really was the devil. When Carly first started complaining about her, I thought she was exaggerating. After meeting her a few times, I now think she was downplaying it. My mom is the master of the subtle insult. This woman is just flat out mean.

"Where is she?" I cast my gaze around the room wildly. I wondered, briefly, if I could escape the bridal shop without being seen.

Carly must have read my mind. "Don't you even think about leaving me alone with that woman."

"I think I forgot to add something to my story," I lied.

"You did not. Don't be a pain in the ass."

Crap.

"Oh, I see she finally arrived." The voice was like nails on a chalkboard. I had only met Kyle's mom, Harriet, a few times. Her voice was the stuff of nightmares, though. That clipped, disapproving tone could shrivel the balls of an elephant.

I turned stiffly and took in Harriet. She was in all her glory – again. She was wearing a pressed pink suit that looked like something she had found at a garage sale at Elizabeth Taylor's house. She was a painfully thin woman, with chalk white skin and pale rose lips. Her makeup was perfect – as usual – and her short brown pageboy was impeccably coiffed. There wasn't a hair out of place.

I caught a glimpse of myself in one of the shop's many mirrors. My shoulder length blonde hair looked like it had been through a wind tunnel. I swallowed hard. "Hello Mrs. Profit," I forced out. "It is so good to see you again."

"I'm sure it is, dear," she clucked. "I told you to call me Harriet. You are Carly's best friend, after all. I wasn't impressed with that fact, as you know, but my son seems genuinely fond of you, so you can't be that bad."

I wondered, briefly, if she would feel the same way if I shoved my new Converse up her ass. Carly pushed me forward. "She's here to make sure the dress fits," Carly said.

"Yes," I lied. "I'm looking forward to it."

Carly narrowed her eyes at me. She could tell I was lying. I doubted the ever oblivious Harriet Profit was aware of that fact, though. Even if she was, I had a hard time caring. If I never saw this woman again after the wedding, I would consider myself lucky.

"It's a beautiful dress," Harriet admitted. "Carly did a good job picking it out."

Carly basked in the momentary moment. This woman rarely had anything nice to say about her.

"Of course," Harriet continued. "You should have probably taken Avery's body type into consideration when you picked the dress."

What did that mean?

Carly narrowed her eyes dangerously. "What did you just say?" Carly may have been desperate to please this woman, but she was loyal to a fault. She could badmouth me all she wanted, but if anyone else did it they should be ready to have their eyes clawed out.

Harriet pursed her lips. "I wasn't saying anything bad," she countered. "She's just a little hippy. She can't help it. It was the way she was born."

I think Harriet thought she was being nice. Carly disagreed. "She's not hippy. She's perfectly healthy."

Harriet looked me up and down dubiously. I could tell she wanted to argue the point, but she wasn't going to fight in public. Harriet was all about outward appearances.

Despite the fighting stance she had taken, Carly decided to let it go – for now. I had no doubt this was going to become a "thing" later that night. Carly pushed me towards the changing room, shoving the lilac monstrosity in my hand as I went. "Don't dawdle in there," she warned me. "Let's just get this over with. If you draw this out longer than you need to, I'm not going to be happy."

I couldn't agree more. I slipped into the dress, glancing at myself in the mirror and grimacing. Now that Harriet had called me hippy, that was all I could focus on. Great. Something new to obsess about.

I stepped out of the dressing room and found Carly sitting in a chair outside. She was randomly shooting a series of patented glares in Harriet's direction when she was sure the older woman wasn't looking.

Harriet turned when she heard the sound of the curtain being pulled back. "It fits," she sighed in relief.

"Why wouldn't it?"

"Well, Carly says you like to eat, so I was a little worried they would have to let the dress out."

It's not like I eat a cow everyday. The first dress fitting had been a month ago. It's not like I'd ballooned into a beach ball in the intervening weeks. Carly got to her feet and regarded me with a genuine smile. "You look great," she exhaled in relief.

I narrowed my eyes as I regarded her. "Did you think it wouldn't fit, too?"

"No," Carly hastily responded. "I just wanted to make sure the dress looked as good in person as it did in my mind."

What a liar.

"You look really good," she repeated.

"Yes," Harriet agreed. "The color really suits your skin tone. You look so much better now that your garish tan is fading."

I hadn't been insulted this much since my mother had seen my new "Fuck you, you fucking fuck" shirt from *The Girl With the Dragon Tattoo*.

"Can I take this off now?" I couldn't get out of this shop quick enough at this point.

"Of course, dear," Harriet waved me off. I saw her glance slip to my *Goonies* socks and the slight, almost imperceptible shake of her head.

I quickly slipped back into my jeans, T-shirt and hoodie and exited the store with the dress in my hand. I had already paid for it -- $250 that I would have much rather spent on new Converse and video games – and I was ready to get out of this hellish situation.

I froze when I heard Harriet start talking to Carly a few feet away. "What are you going to do for shoes?"

"We're having heels dyed," Carly said.

This was the first I had heard of that. "Those ugly satiny ones you showed me? I didn't agree to that."

"You'll be fine," Carly shushed me.

"How do you even know what size shoes I wear?"

"You have huge feet. You're always complaining about how huge your feet are. You've got seventy pairs of shoes in your laundry room – and they're all the same size – stop being ridiculous."

"I'm changing into something comfortable at the reception," I grumbled under my breath.

"I'm sure the dress will look great with canvas high tops," Harriet clucked sarcastically.

If I had a hammer, I'd totally throw it at her right now.

Five

Harriet left the store before Carly. I could tell Carly wanted to talk to me – but I wasn't all that happy with her right now. Dyed lilac shoes? Would I ever live down the shame?

Carly knew I was agitated. She led me outside before I lost it.

"Were you just going to spring those shoes on me the day of the wedding?" I was incredulous.

"Basically," Carly admitted. "I knew you would never agree to wear them. I figured you'd take one look at me in my white dress and not be able to tell me no."

Well, at least she was honest.

"I don't want to wear dyed shoes."

"You can take them off and go barefoot after the photos have been taken."

"Photos!"

Carly bit the inside of her cheek. "Of course there will be photos. Don't be purposely obtuse. You knew there would be photos."

"Will the shoes be in them?"

"Only a few."

I blew out a sigh. "How long until the wedding?"

"A little less than a month."

"No offense, but I'm ready for it to be over with."

"You and me both. The less I have to see of that woman, the better," Carly said bitterly.

"We could smother her in her sleep," I offered.

"We would get caught. I would be the first suspect and Jake would know you wouldn't let me commit a murder on my own."

She had a point.

When Carly was sure that I was sufficiently calm – or as calm as I was going to get in the next hour – she said her goodbyes and left me fuming on the street. I was so caught up in my righteous indignation, I didn't notice a pair of feet stop next to me on the street corner.

"Is this a private freak out, or can anyone join in?"

I jumped when I heard the voice. I recognized it. I didn't even have to look up to know that I would find Eliot standing next to me.

I plastered a fake bright smile on my face and met his gaze. He looked as good as I remembered. His shoulder-length brown hair was glinting under the sunlight and his rich brown eyes were filled with amusement as he regarded me. "I'm not freaking out," I lied.

"Then what are you doing?"

"Contemplating the meaning of life?"

"And?"

"And? And it sucks." Seriously, dyed shoes are just embarrassing.

"Well, I can't argue with that," Eliot's smile was fairly welcoming. I took that as a good sign.

"How are you?" I bit the bullet. We might as well have the uncomfortable conversation that was bubbling under the surface. At least, when it was over, I would have a better understanding of where I stood.

"I'm fine," he said. "No long-lasting injuries."

"That's good," I offered lamely.

"How are you?" The question was pointed.

"I'm fine."

Eliot looked up at the bridal store behind me. There was a question in his eyes. I wasn't sure if he actually wanted to ask it, though.

"I was getting fitted for my bridesmaid dress for Carly's wedding," I explained hurriedly. I lifted up the lilac sheath, which was covered in a plastic dress bag, as proof.

"I was wondering," Eliot laughed. "I didn't think you and Jake would make a rush for the aisle that quickly."

What? "I don't . . . what?"

"You and Jake. I figured you'd made up. That was why I hadn't heard from you." Eliot steadfastly averted his gaze from mine.

"Jake and I are not together," I said. "Why would you think that?"

"Because you just disappeared after you came and saw me at the hospital." There was a certain edge of frustration laced throughout Eliot's words.

"I did go back," I protested. "You were already discharged. I figured you would call me when you were feeling better but . . . it never happened."

Eliot smiled to himself, the first real smile today. "Do you have one of those phones that only receives calls?"

"No. I just figured you would call me if you wanted to talk to me."

"And I figured you would call me if you wanted to talk to me."

Eliot and I both burst out in laughter. It was a surreal situation. We lapsed into silence when our giggles had subsided. Eliot broke the silence. "So you're not with Jake?"

"Of course not," I scoffed. I didn't tell him that I hadn't talked to Jake since that day in the hospital either.

"Well, I'm glad to hear that," Eliot said honestly. "I was hoping that maybe . . . " He broke off uncertainly.

"Maybe what?" I prodded.

Eliot swallowed hard. He was clearly waging an internal battle in his own mind. "Do you want to have dinner with me?" He asked finally.

I was surprised – and thrilled. "I would like that," I said honestly. The sense of relief that was washing over me was a surprise – even to me. It was like the stress I had been carrying for the past month was just erased. Sure, my boss still hated me and

Jake was avoiding me like the plague, but the Eliot situation was definitely looking up.

Eliot seemed equally relieved by my response. "Really? This would be a real date, you know?"

"I figured," I said sarcastically.

Eliot paused a second, then he fixed me with a hard look. "If I'm going to date you, then I'm going to date you."

"Isn't that how dating usually works?"

"For normal people," Eliot replied. "You're not normal, though."

"I'm better than normal," I teased.

"You are. You're also frustrating – and you don't listen for shit."

The warm glow I had felt when Eliot asked me out was starting to fade. "Are you asking me out or insulting me?"

"Both. Get used to it."

"When do you want to have dinner?" I didn't want the invitation to just sit out there and ferment. I wanted a definite plan of action. I was ready to move forward for a change.

"What are you doing tonight?"

Tonight? He was as eager as I was. "Nothing," I said hastily.

"Well, then let's go out tonight."

I remembered my mom's call from earlier in the day and slapped myself in the forehead. "Oh, I can't."

Eliot regarded me suspiciously. "Why?"

"Family dinner," I explained.

"Family dinner?" Eliot looked confused.

"Once a week, I have to drive up to my family's restaurant in Oakland County and have dinner with all of them. I've missed the last two weeks. If I don't go tonight my mom will send out a search party – and it will be a really shrill and loud search party."

Eliot smiled despite himself. "Well, I guess that's a good enough reason."

I was mentally toying with an idea. I couldn't tell if it was a good idea or not, but I didn't want to lose the forward momentum I was feeling. "You could come with me, if you want." I had said it relatively quietly. I think Eliot was surprised by the invitation.

"Go to family dinner with you?"

"Yeah," I plowed on. "It's not a big deal. It's pretty casual."

"Define casual." Now Eliot was the one who was hedging.

"We have a family table at the restaurant," I explained. "All my aunts, uncles and cousins will be there."

"And your mom?" Eliot looked dubious.

"And my mom."

"I don't know . . . " Eliot looked torn.

"You don't have to. It was just an idea." I averted my gaze from Eliot.

He regarded me for a second. "Why not."

"Really?"

"Yeah," Eliot said. "I'll have to meet them eventually. They're just normal people, right?"

Define normal. "Of course."

"And they'll like me, right?"

I looked at his long hair, white tank top, flannel shirt and the Native American tattoos on his forearms and realized one thing with absolute certainty: My mom was going to hate him on sight.

"They'll love you."

Six

Eliot insisted on driving to dinner – even though he had never been to the family restaurant before. I don't think he trusted my driving. The last time he had been near me when I was behind the wheel I had accidentally hit him with my car. Personally, I blame him for running into the middle of the road. I don't think he felt the same way, though.

The restaurant itself was located an hour north of Detroit, in an area of Oakland County that was still more rural than urban. My great-grandmother had started it in the 1960s, and she had passed it down to her son – my grandfather. My grandfather was still technically in charge, but he had passed on the day-to-day operations to my Uncle Tim. My grandfather still went to the restaurant everyday, but it was usually to just hold court with the regular coffee drinkers that frequented the establishment.

It was a real family endeavor – with much of the family still working there. The décor was basic, and the booths vinyl. I found it warm and inviting, but I was curious about how Eliot would see it.

For his part, Eliot seemed to be getting increasingly nervous during the drive. He kept asking me pointed questions about my family.

"So, you're an only child but you have a lot of cousins, right?"

"Right."

"And you're all close?"

"Right."

"Will Lexie be there?"

That was a good question. Eliot had met Lexie when she had been living with me a few weeks ago. It was his idea for her to go to rehab – a move she had initially fought. Eliot didn't overtly dislike Lexie, but he wasn't exactly fond of her either. He thought she spent too much time flitting from thing to thing – and leeching off whatever person was most convenient at that point in her life.

"I don't know. Last time I heard, she was still in rehab."

"She should stay there," I heard him mutter.

"Don't say that in front of my family. They'll lynch you."

Eliot looked at me out of the corner of his eye. I had a sneaking suspicion he was starting to rethink family dinner. It was too late for that, though.

"Will Derrick be there?"

My cousin Derrick, Lexie's brother, was a sheriff's deputy in Macomb County. He worked for Jake. We were close in age, which meant we usually fought like brother and sister. Between Lexie and I, Derrick was constantly being teased by his co-workers.

"Probably."

"Will he have that television reporter with him?"

Much to my disdain, Derrick had started dating a television reporter from Channel 4 about five weeks ago. I had thought he was doing it to irritate me at first, but they were still going strong. I still couldn't stand her.

"Probably," I growled.

Eliot smirked. "You still don't like her?"

"No."

"What's your mom do?"

"She's a teacher." Which was probably why she was always treating me like I was in the fifth grade.

"And your dad?"

"He's a businessman, but he won't be there. My parents are divorced."

Eliot seemed relieved by that little tidbit. I didn't blame him. My mom was going to be bad enough. My dad would take one look at him and think he was a dirty hippie, though. That was a bridge we would have to cross at a later date. Thankfully, my dad traveled a lot.

When we got to town, I directed Eliot to the family restaurant. When we exited his Range Rover, I could see that the nervousness had returned. "It's going to be fine," I promised. I was mostly certain of that. "We're a lot harder on each other than we are on newcomers."

Eliot looked slightly placated.

"Of course," I continued. "You're the first guy I've brought to family dinner since I was a teenager. So they'll probably look at you like you're a circus freak and expect you to perform on command."

Eliot groaned. "Did Jake come to these?"

"Yeah," I admitted reluctantly.

"Were they nice to him?"

"Yeah," I said blithely. "Of course, he knew them because we grew up together."

"You're not making me feel any better."

"You'll be fine." I waved off Eliot's concerns. I had my own problems to worry about. The truth was, I was happy Eliot would be there because it might stop my mom from railing at me in front of everyone for missing two family dinners in a row.

Eliot was still standing on his side of his truck. I could tell he was debating about getting in it and driving away — leaving me to deal with my family alone. I stalked to the other side of the vehicle, grabbed his hand, and started dragging him towards the front door.

Eliot let himself be led. Given his impressive muscle mass, I couldn't have actually made him move otherwise.

When we entered the restaurant, I greeted Eva, one of the longtime waitresses, with a friendly nod.

"It's a good thing you're hear," she trilled. "If you had missed another dinner you probably would have been on the menu next week."

She was probably right.

Eliot was gripping my hand hard. I thought his terror at meeting my family was actually pretty cute. He was a former Army Ranger, after all. He had faced down terrorists and crazed soldiers – but my family was causing him to quake in his stylish cowboy boots.

I led Eliot to the family booth. I was relieved to see that my mom hadn't arrived yet. The family booth is one of those long, rectangular tables made up of three eating surfaces – with gaps in between. Derrick was sitting at the far end. I slid into the booth next to him, making sure to leave room for Eliot on the end.

Derrick looked surprised when he saw Eliot. "You brought reinforcements, I see." He nodded at Eliot in greeting. I had no idea how well they knew each other. I did know, though, that Derrick would be telling Jake about this. That was an uncomfortable conversation in the making.

"Don't be a pain," I admonished Derrick. "Where is everyone?" I looked around the table. Only two of my cousins were there – Mario and Justin. They were busy talking to each other, though, and not paying attention to anyone else.

"Upstairs," Derrick supplied. "In the apartment."

The second floor of the restaurant was actually a really nice two-bedroom apartment. Through the years, pretty much everyone in the family had lived in the apartment at one time or another. To my knowledge, it had been empty for the last six months.

"Why?"

"Sally is moving up there."

My Aunt Sally was one of the free spirits in my family. She was on her second husband, after her first one turned out to be gay.

Two of her kids were fully grown, but she had a 10-year-old daughter with her second husband.

"Why is Sally moving up there?"

"She's leaving Steve."

Steve was Sally's second husband. In her zest to make sure she didn't marry another homosexual, she had married an overt redneck the second time around. I missed the gay guy. He was a lot more fun.

"Why?" Personally, I never understood why she married Steve in the first place. I'm guessing her surprise pregnancy in her thirties had a lot to do with it. My grandfather had spent weeks lamenting the fact that a grown woman didn't know how to use birth control.

"Wouldn't you leave him?" Derrick wasn't fond of Steve either.

"I never would have married him."

I took the time to explain the Sally and Steve information to Eliot. My family used to embarrass me when I was a teenager. Now I just find them funny. Eliot merely shook his head. "You have an interesting gene pool, don't you?"

"You have no idea," Derrick answered for me. "Half the family should be committed and the other half should be locked up."

"Where do you fall in that scenario?" I asked him.

"I'm the only normal one."

Right.

Family members were slowly starting to descend from upstairs. My aunts Sally and Marnie were in deep conversation when they got to the table. "I'm going to go up there and paint tomorrow."

"Why are you going to paint? It looks fine."

"I don't like the color."

They both pulled up short when they caught sight of Eliot. He didn't exactly fit in. I could see a miasma of thoughts flitting through their minds. Marnie was the first to speak. "Who is this?"

I introduced Eliot, who got to his feet to shake both their hands. Derrick was watching the scene with a mixture of bemusement and genuine curiosity. "I can't wait until your mom sees him."

When Marnie realized whom Eliot was, and that he was the one who had been responsible for directing her daughter, Lexie, towards rehab, she warmed to him considerably.

The bell above the front door dinged and I looked up to see my mom entering. She hadn't seen me yet. I braced myself. Eliot had settled back in the booth next to me. "My mom is here."

Eliot looked up at the door, taking in my mom's blonde hair and blue eyes, and smiled. "You look like her."

"I do not."

"You do, too."

"If you want to get into her pants, I wouldn't keep saying that," Derrick warned Eliot sternly.

"Why?"

"Let's just say that's not the way to her heart," Derrick laughed. "It might be the way to her future ulcer, though."

Eliot regarded me for a second. "You guys should have your own reality show."

My mom froze when she got to the table and her eyes found Eliot. She met my gaze for a second and I plastered my patented fake smile on my face. "Hi, mom! This is Eliot."

I practically yelled the statement. I have no idea why. I guess I was nervous, too.

"The pawnshop owner?"

Eliot got to his feet again and extended his hand to my mom. She took it stiffly. Even though I could tell she was freaked out by his looks, she was nothing if not polite. "It's nice to meet you."

"You, too." If Eliot was nervous, he didn't show it. He sat down next to me again, but his gaze never left my mom's face.

For her part, my mom was stoic. She slid into the booth and positioned herself at the middle table. "I'm glad you could come," she said. "I assume you're the reason my daughter missed the last two dinners. She was afraid to introduce you to us? Was that the reason?"

"No ma'am," Eliot said amiably. "This is our first date."

I couldn't help but snicker to myself. Eliot was utilizing my own defense mechanism. He was poking the mommy bear with a stick to see if she would bite.

To her credit, my mom didn't take the bait. "I'm just glad she finally brought a man – even if he does have long hair. I was starting to think she was a lesbian."

Derrick barked out a laugh beside me. I elbowed him sharply. "Ow." He rubbed his ribcage and shot me a dark look. "This is why she thinks you're a lesbian. You hit when you should be using your words. A proper lady would use words instead of fists."

"Shut up."

"He has a point," my mom chided me.

Dinner had a more relaxed feel after that. We ordered. I opted for my grandpa's famous vegetable soup and a BLT, while Eliot stuck to a burger and fries like Derrick. I don't think he wanted to rock the boat.

"This is really good," Eliot said after we'd been eating in silence for a few minutes.

"I'm glad to see you're not a vegetarian," my mom said.

"Nope, not a vegetarian," Eliot replied.

"I wasn't sure because of your tattoos."

"Why would his tattoos mean he was a vegetarian?" I asked irritably.

"You know, that's how people are these days."

"Avery has two tattoos and she's not a vegetarian." This time, Derrick managed to shift and avoid the blow I aimed at his mid-section.

My mom was eying me incredulously. "You have tattoos?"

"No," I lied.

"Yes she does," Derrick said. "She's got a turtle and some *Lord of the Rings* thing."

"You have a *Lord of the Rings* tattoo?" Eliot looked interested. "Where?"

"On my shoulder blade," I muttered.

"Sounds hot," he laughed.

I could tell he was making fun of me, so I ignored him.

Thankfully, the conversation at the table turned to Sally's new living arrangements. "Why did you leave Steve?"

My mom gave me a dirty look. She vacillates between the belief that you shouldn't air your dirty laundry in public to garrulous gossip.

"He's obnoxious," Sally answered.

He was obnoxious when she married him. "So, what else is new?"

"He told me he doesn't think women should work."

"What should we do? Clean the house and pop out babies?" I was joking.

"Yes," Sally said seriously.

"He's a douche," I supplied.

"Avery! Don't use language like that," my mom snapped.

I could feel Eliot shaking with silent laughter next me.

"I'm going to need help moving tomorrow afternoon," Sally announced.

I noticed that everyone at the table had went unusually silent. No one wanted to help.

"Do you have to work tomorrow?" My mom asked.

"No," I hedged. "But I rode with Eliot and he's got to work tomorrow and he's my ride home." She couldn't possibly argue with that.

"I don't have to work tomorrow," Eliot answered.

"You don't want to drive back out here tomorrow, though, do you?" I was giving him an out. Why wasn't he taking it?

"I can just get a hotel room here." His eyes were twinkling. He was doing this on purpose.

"Or you could just stay in the apartment upstairs?" Sally offered warmly.

"That sounds great," Eliot enthused. "I would be happy to help."

He wasn't so cute anymore.

"Avery can come and stay at the house with me," my mom interjected.

Yeah, that wasn't going to happen. "I don't want to leave Eliot alone in a strange environment. I better stay upstairs with him."

Eliot looked intrigued by the prospect. I was suddenly nervous again.

My mom opened her mouth to argue but Marnie stepped in instead. "Oh, give it up, she's an adult. If she wants to have sex she's going to have sex. You're not going to stop her."

I could feel my cheeks starting to burn with embarrassment. Everyone at the table was now staring at Eliot and me.

"I bet you wished you were a lesbian about now?"

I slammed my foot down on Derrick's, which was resting next to mine underneath the table. "Shut up."

"What? I was just saying what everyone at this table was thinking."

He wasn't wrong.

Seven

Throughout the rest of dinner, I felt decidedly uncomfortable. If Eliot was feeling the same thing, he hid it well. I had spent the night with Eliot before, and nothing had happened. Of course, I had hit him with a car one of those times – and forced him to sleep on the couch the other. I knew he would be a gentleman if I wanted him to be – but I wasn't sure I wanted him to be one this time.

I couldn't really give too much thought to my predicament. My mom was giving me dirty looks from down the table, and they were starting to get to me. After dinner –which I stretched out by having a hot fudge sundae – my family began to disperse and leave the restaurant.

Sally lingered, saying she would be back early the next morning because she wanted to paint the apartment before we started moving stuff up. "I figured I would come over here and paint first and you guys could go help load the truck while I'm doing that."

I couldn't help but wonder if this whole "painting" thing wasn't an elaborate ruse to get out of the heavy lifting associated with moving – but I didn't say that out loud. I had other things on my mind, at this point anyway. Tomorrow might be a different story.

After a few minutes, only Eliot and my mom were left. She was still giving me "the look." You know the one. The one that says "I'm really disappointed in you and I know what you're going to do tonight." I ignored it.

I said goodbye to my mom and led Eliot through the back of the restaurant. I didn't turn around to see if she was still watching us.

There are two ways to get into the apartment above the restaurant. One is a stairwell off of the kitchen. The other is a wood walkway outside that leads up to the sliding glass doors in the kitchen. No one ever uses the wooden staircase – mostly because there's a question about whether or not you'll plunge to your death if you do.

When we got upstairs, Eliot looked around in surprise. "This is actually pretty nice," he said.

"It is," I agreed.

The apartment had two bedrooms – one at each end of the apartment. There was one bathroom at the far end, near the smaller of the two bedrooms, and a wide and expansive living room. The kitchen was adjacent to the living room; you just had to take a step up. It was kind of like the letter "L."

"Have you ever lived here?" Eliot asked.

"Yeah, twice. Once when I was a kid and my parents were waiting for our house to be ready. That was only for a couple of weeks. Then I lived here with Derrick for the summer before we went to college. Neither one of us wanted to live at home and this was our next best option."

"Why didn't you want to live at home?"

"You've met my mom. Imagine what she was like when she still thought she had an inkling of control over me. It was ugly."

"Yeah," Eliot chuckled. "She's a little intense. Is she like this with everyone – or do I just rub her the wrong way?"

"Don't take it personally," I admonished him, climbing up into the kitchen and sitting at the small rectangular table. It was the only furniture currently in the apartment. "She can't help herself. She doesn't see herself as being oppressive."

"Oppressive?" Eliot raised his eyebrows as he regarded me. "That's an odd word to describe your mom."

I shrugged noncommittally. "She's just a control freak. She doesn't see it. There's no way to change it."

"So how do you handle it?"

"I purposely try to make her head implode," I replied simply.

"That doesn't seem like it is much of an endeavor."

"Most of the time, it's not."

Eliot eyed me speculatively for a few minutes and then turned back to the empty apartment. "Where are we going to sleep?"

"I think there are some sleeping bags in the closet," I offered.

Eliot wandered over to the small closet beside the bathroom and opened the door. I could hear him chuckling to himself. I remained sitting until he walked back into the living room and held up two sleeping bags. One of them was *Star Wars* and the other was *G.I. Joe*. "I'm guessing the *Star Wars* one belonged to you, but who was the *G.I. Joe* fanatic?"

"Derrick," I said simply. "Our interests as kids were somewhat limited. We spent a lot of time in the woods with paintball guns – and our imaginations."

"You two were close?"

"Yeah, we're only nine months apart in age."

"Are you still close?"

I shrugged. "As close as we can be. I can't imagine it's easy to have me as a cousin – especially when you work for the police."

"I guess," Eliot said. "I think you two are kind of funny. You act more like brother and sister than anything else."

"We were essentially raised together," I said.

"Is he close with Lexie?"

"No," I shook my head. "If I'm embarrassing, Lexie is mortifying."

"I see that," Eliot said.

He started spreading the sleeping bags out on the floor, tossing two pillows he found in the closet on the floor next to them. He plopped down on the *G.I. Joe* one, pulling his boots off and placing them against the wall as he did.

I watched him curiously. "Why did you volunteer us to stay here?" I finally asked.

"Why not?"

"It just seems odd," I admitted. "Like you're trying too hard for them to like you."

"You think this was about them liking me?" Eliot looked surprised.

"It wasn't?"

"It was about irritating you – and maybe getting you alone." The look Eliot slid towards me was predatory – and sexy.

"You knew that we'd end up alone up here?" Somehow, I doubted that.

"No," Eliot admitted. "I thought we'd end up in a hotel – but this is just as good."

"Yeah, childhood sleeping bags and a hard floor are definitely sexy," I teased.

"Sexy is a state of mind, not your surroundings," Eliot leaned back against the wall. There was a about twenty feet between us – but it felt like I could feel his warmth emanating from here.

"You seem pretty sure that you're going to get lucky," I said, licking my lips nervously.

"I wouldn't want to disappoint your mom," he laughed.

That was only a plus from my perspective. I slowly got up and moved towards him. What the hell, right?

∞

I woke up in a tangle of arms, legs and *Star Wars* fabric. I could feel Eliot curled up behind me, with his right arm wrapped around me tightly. He felt me stir and snuggled in closer to me, mumbling into my tangled blonde hair as he did. "Good morning."

"Morning," I murmured back, relaxing back into his strong arms for a few minutes. I looked up at the sliding glass doors in the kitchen and saw that the light was starting to filter in. It was almost dawn. Sally would be here soon. And, as comfortable and relaxed as I felt, I knew that if Eliot and I were found naked and wrapped in my childhood sleeping bag – things would get unpleasant, to say the least.

"We have to get up," I said reluctantly.

"I know," Eliot said. He kissed my temple quickly and then climbed up. I took a second to appreciate his naked rear end before I started getting dressed, too. I only had the same clothes I had worn the day before, so it didn't take very long. I excused myself to go into the bathroom and ran my fingers through my hair. It was a losing battle.

I asked Eliot to bring my purse into the bathroom for me. Luckily, I had an extra hairbrush inside of it. I wet it under the faucet and ran it through my hair. It wasn't a vast improvement, but it was better than it had been. I threw all of my hair into a pony tail and then splashed some water on my face.

When I came back out into the living room, Eliot had folded up the sleeping bags and stashed them back into the linen closet. Despite the fact that we'd had a, um, rigorous evening, Eliot's hair barely looked out of place. I handed him the hairbrush anyway and watched as he disappeared into the bathroom.

When he was done, Eliot came back out into the living room and shrugged into his flannel shirt. He then turned to me expectantly. A memory of last night rushed into my head and I could feel my face flush.

Eliot smirked when he saw the reddening of my cheeks. "Are you regretting it now?"

"No," I admitted. "I just know my mom is going to take one look at me and know the dirty, dirty things we did last night."

"Do you think she'll really care?"

"Oh, yeah, it's going to totally piss her off," I responded.

"Is that a bad thing or a good thing?"

"It's a good thing," I said. "It's definitely a good thing."

Eliot held his hand out to me and I took it, letting him pull me towards him and brush a soft kiss across my lips. Inviting him to dinner really was one of my better ideas – and that's saying something, because I'm something of a genius (especially in my own mind).

Eliot and I heard someone outside of the apartment door and I inadvertently took a step back. I wasn't surprised to see Sally standing there. She was laden down with painting supplies.

"Oh, good, you're up," she said. She was eying us both speculatively for a minute. I could tell she wanted to find out if anything happened – but she currently had other things on her mind. That would have to wait.

"We're going to go down to the restaurant and have breakfast and then we'll go help pack your stuff," I said.

"Good," she said. "By the time you get back here I should be done painting."

I led Eliot back downstairs. My cousin Mario was cooking this morning and he looked surprised when he saw Eliot and I descend from the upstairs apartment. "Looks like someone got lucky last night," he teased.

Mario was seven years younger than me and fresh out of high school. He was working at the restaurant while he put himself through college. He was one of my funnier cousins – but I wasn't especially in the mood for his brand of humor this morning.

"Are you jealous?"

"Hell yes," Mario answered amiably. "He's very pretty. His hair looks like it feels like spun satin."

Mario has a weird sense of humor.

Eliot and I went back out to the dining room and slid into the family booth. Derrick was already eating his breakfast. I was surprised to see him. "What are you doing here? I thought you were going back to the city?"

"I was," Derrick grumbled.

"Did they nag you until you agreed to come back?"

"No," Derrick said. "My mom nagged me so I spent the night at her house. On the couch."

My family is a little co-dependent.

I ordered eggs, hash browns, ham, wheat toast and tomato juice – my favorite breakfast. Eliot ordered pancakes. When the waitress left, I turned back to Derrick. "How long do you think this is going to take?"

"Knowing Sally? All day. It's not exactly how I wanted to spend my Saturday," he grumbled. "I wanted to spend the afternoon with Devon."

Ah, Devon, his Channel 4 sweetie. Good. I didn't like her anyway.

"She's hot," Eliot said to Derrick as a means of conversation.

I glared at Eliot disdainfully. "You're much hotter, baby," he absentmindedly patted my hand as he sipped from his cup of coffee.

Derrick snickered and sipped from his own cup of coffee. He was now looking at me curiously. "Your mom is going to know you got laid last night," he said finally.

"I don't know what you're talking about," I lied, staring down at my silverware.

Derrick smirked. "You kind of have a glow." He turned to Eliot. "Good job. Maybe she'll be more interested in you than fucking up my job for awhile."

"I don't fuck up your job," I argued.

"You don't make it any easier," he countered.

Thankfully, my breakfast had arrived so I had something else to focus on besides popping Derrick's head like a really big zit. I found that I was suddenly ravenous. Derrick watched me dunk my toast in my egg yolks and started laughing. "He took a lot of out you, huh? You need some nourishment?"

I glanced over at Eliot, but he apparently wasn't going to ride to my rescue. "Do you want to chime in here?"

"Nope." Eliot took a big bite of his pancakes and smirked at me.

So much for my white knight.

Eight

The rest of breakfast was spent in relative silence. The conversation we did have revolved around Sarah Frank and her mysterious disappearance. "Have you heard anything?" I asked Derrick.

"Nothing more than you've already been told," Derrick answered succinctly.

How did he know what I'd been told? "I think you guys know more than you're saying," I said.

"Why would you say that?"

That's an evasion. When you answer a question with a question that means you're hiding something. "Because I think it's weird that the sheriff's department would have a press conference at the home of a missing woman."

"Why is that weird?" Eliot asked.

"It's just not normal."

"You're the last person that should be judging what is normal," Derrick sniped.

"See, that's another evasion," I countered. "I know you're lying to me. I know you're all lying to me. I'm going to find out what you're hiding."

"Shouldn't you be focusing on your new boyfriend?" Derrick may be a master manipulator, but I was better.

"I'm a consummate multi-tasker," I said.

"Lucky for you," Derrick told Eliot.

"I do feel lucky," Eliot said finally. "She's never boring."

I smirked at Derrick triumphantly.

"That was a backhanded compliment," Derrick said. "He's saying you make him want to pull his own hair out."

"That's not what he said."

"That's what he meant."

"It is not."

"It is, too."

I turned to Eliot. "That's not what you meant, is it?"

Eliot swallowed the bite of pancakes he'd been chewing. "I meant what I said. You're never boring."

Derrick barked out a laugh. "See."

I finished up my breakfast in a moody silence. If Eliot was bothered by my sudden sullenness, he didn't acknowledge it.

The sound of the bell ringing above the door caught all of our attention, and we all turned to see who was arriving. I could only hope it was karma – and she was coming to give Derrick a good swift kick in the ass.

Instead it was my conscience coming to give me a bitter dose of reality in the form of my mother. She was heading straight towards us.

"Good morning," Eliot greeted her amiably.

"Good morning," my mom said stiffly. I noticed that my grandfather had come out into the main room from the kitchen. He slipped into the booth at the far end of the table and was eating his morning breakfast. My grandfather was a big guy – and he loved his food. "Good morning, grandpa," I greeted him.

"Morning, Dolly," he said.

My grandfather calls all of his granddaughters Dolly. I have no idea why.

"Who is your friend?"

I introduced Eliot. My grandfather hadn't had a chance to meet him the night before. My mom had slid into the middle section of the booth and was sitting next to Derrick. She picked a piece of toast off his plate and started nibbling on it. Derrick gave her a dirty look. "Do you want your own breakfast?"

"No," she sighed. "I'll just have this piece of toast."

"Maybe I wanted that piece of toast," Derrick countered.

"You've had enough," she responded.

I pursed my lips and smirked at Derrick. When he was sure my mom wasn't looking, he shot me the finger.

My grandfather was still staring at Eliot thoughtfully. "Is he your boyfriend?"

I cast a sideways glance at Eliot. We really hadn't defined that.

"Yes, sir," Eliot answered for me.

"You are?" I was surprised at how quickly he had answered the question.

Eliot ignored me.

"Shouldn't you have decided that before last night?" Derrick asked.

If my legs were long enough to reach him, I would have kicked him. "Eat your breakfast," I admonished him.

My mom was fixing her icy glare on me again. Great.

"So, I figured we would all go over to Sally's now." What? I can divert, too.

"What did you do last night?" My mom's tone was no-nonsense.

"Should we all leave now?" I ignored her question.

"What did you do last night?" She's like a dog with a bone, I swear.

"We slept." That's not a lie. We did sleep. After.

"In separate rooms?"

"Yes," I lied.

I could see Eliot shaking his head out of the corner of his eye. He was absolutely no help.

"She's lying," Derrick supplied. I really hate him sometimes.

"Are you lying?" My mom's voice had risen an octave.

"Who are you going to believe?" That was a loaded question.

"Just leave her alone," my grandfather chimed in. "She's an adult. At least we know she's not a lesbian now – even if that fellow does have some mighty long hair for a boy."

Eliot ran his fingers through his hair self-consciously. I moved to push him out of the booth. "We'll meet you over at Sally's."

My grandfather got up from the table. "I'm going to run upstairs and go to the bathroom and then I'll meet you over there."

That was code. He really means he's going to sit on the toilet upstairs until he's sure we're all gone and then get caught up in some work task that conveniently keeps him from helping us.

He disappeared into the kitchen. He really wouldn't be a lot of help anyway. He would probably be more of a hindrance, barking out orders and directing everyone else to do things until everything resulted in a really large clusterfuck.

My mom was still regarding Eliot and I suspiciously. "What?" I turned to her in exasperation.

"Nothing," she pursed her lips.

"Just let it go," I grumbled.

"You let it go," she countered.

The whole family devolves into middle school comebacks sometimes. Luckily for us, things didn't have a chance to sink to any new lows because there were raised voices emanating from the kitchen.

The other customers in the restaurant were looking beyond the swinging double doors curiously. Derrick and I pushed through the doors and followed the ruckus. Eliot and my mom were a few paces behind.

The voices were loud – and familiar.

"What the hell are you doing? Is this some type of whorehouse?" My grandfather was bellowing from the top of the stairs.

I raced up the stairs to see what kind of situation had suddenly evolved. I was shocked to find my aunt Sally cowering on the floor. She was shirtless – and she was trying to cover herself.

"What's going on?"

"I was painting," Sally gasped; reaching for the tarp she had placed on the floor to protect it from the paint.

"Naked! She was painting naked," my grandfather was beside himself with disbelief.

"I didn't want to ruin my clothes," Sally said lamely.

I felt a warm body move in behind me and turned to see Eliot taking in the scene with a small smile.

"Like I said, you're never boring."

Nine

I left my mom and grandfather to deal with the naked painting incident. This is why you don't live in a place where you have no privacy – or where family can just wander in unannounced.

"Why didn't you lock the door?" I heard my mom ask disgustedly. She's always practical.

"I didn't think I needed to," Sally answered.

"You know he needs his bathroom time after breakfast," my mom countered.

"I forgot."

Derrick, Eliot and I descended the stairs and exited the restaurant through the back door. When we got outside, Derrick and I burst out laughing. Eliot watched us curiously.

"I take it this doesn't' surprise you," he said.

"It's not even the weirdest thing Sally has done all week," Derrick answered truthfully.

Eliot and I followed Derrick to Sally's house – which was only a few blocks away. When we pulled up to the house, Eliot seemed surprised. "Why would she move out of this house and into a small apartment?"

Sally's house was beautiful. It was an older, yellow farm house that she had spent a lot of time fixing up and decorating.

"I don't know. Maybe she's scared of Steve."

"Why would she be scared of him?" Eliot looked surprised.

Describing Steve is difficult. He's one of those guys that comes across as amiable, but after talking to him for a few minutes you realize that he's got a lot of old world attitudes. He believes women should cook, clean and shut the hell up. Most women believe that he should just shut the hell up.

"Wouldn't she have known that he was like that before she married him?" Eliot seemed confused.

"She did, but I think she thought she could change him," I offered lamely.

"Well, that's pretty stupid. You can't change someone. They are who they are. You either accept that, or you move on."

"Is that a warning for me?" I asked him curiously.

"No, it was just a reminder to me," he teased.

We got out of the car and joined Derrick on the front lawn. No one else had arrived yet.

"We're fifteen minutes early," Derrick said. "Do you think we should just go inside and start getting stuff?"

"I don't know, " I shrugged. "Is Steve here?"

Derrick nodded his head towards the pickup truck in the driveway. "His truck is here."

We opted to wait until someone with at least a semblance of authority arrived. Thankfully, Marnie and my mom were only a few minutes behind us.

"What are you waiting for?" Marnie chastised us. "Don't just stand there. Start moving stuff."

"We weren't sure if we were allowed to go in the house," Derrick argued.

Marnie waved Derrick's protests off disinterestedly. "Come on."

We started following my mom and Marnie up the porch steps when the side door swung open. Steve was standing in the door with one of his brothers – and they didn't look happy to see us.

"What are you doing here?"

"We're here to get Sally's stuff," Marnie challenged him.

"Well, then you're going to be disappointed."

I saw Derrick and Eliot exchange furtive looks. They clearly sensed this was going to turn into more of a battle than anyone else had anticipated.

Marnie wasn't going to be dissuaded, though. She and Sally fought like cats and dogs – or like sisters that were only eleven months apart in age – but she wasn't going to put up with any of Steve's bullshit. "Get out of the way."

"Sally is not leaving me," Steve argued.

"Then you're going to be disappointed," my mom chimed in.

"A woman does not leave her husband," Steve countered. "I am the head of this house and what I say goes."

I sucked in a breath. Uh-oh.

"The head of the house," Marnie laughed. "You're barely third in line."

Steve opened the door wider and stepped out onto the porch to bar Marnie from going any farther. I saw Derrick tense beside me. Crap.

Eliot took a step forward, and Steve and his brother were suddenly focused on him. He does make an imposing sight.

"Why don't we just talk about this?" I could tell he wasn't exactly interested in getting in a brawl. At least not yet.

"Why don't you go home and braid your hair," Steve countered. His brother high-fived him for his cleverness. Sometimes I wonder if their mother and father were also brother and sister.

"What is it with this family and my hair?" Eliot turned to me.

"I don't know," I admitted. "I like it."

The truth was, I found it sexy as hell. I didn't think now was the time to tell him that, though.

"Can you two stop flirting with each other and focus on the present," Derrick snapped.

I still wasn't sure what the big deal was. It's not like Steve and his brother were some immovable, trained military force.

Eliot seemed to read my mind. "They're not the only ones," he said. "There are at least two more people in the house."

"How do you know?"

"Someone keeps peeking out from that side window," he gestured toward the picture window that was shrouded in curtains. "And someone is pacing in front of that upstairs window."

Whoops. I hadn't noticed that.

"So much for your vaunted powers of observation," Derrick scoffed.

Eliot turned to Derrick. "Are you armed?"

"No. Are you?"

"No."

"Nothing in your car?"

"I didn't think I would need anything. This was just supposed to be a simple family dinner." Eliot seemed calm, but I could tell that his muscles were tensed and ready for action.

"Nothing is ever simple with Avery," Derrick reminded him.

"I should realize that at this point," Eliot ceded.

"How did this become my fault?"

Everyone turned their attention back to the front porch. Steve was regarding Derrick and Eliot, while steadfastly trying to ignore my mom and Marnie. That wasn't going to win him any points.

"You don't have any jurisdiction here," Steve reminded Derrick.

"If I feel that anyone's life is in danger, I do," Derrick countered.

I had noticed that Eliot was slipping away from both of us and making his way towards the front of the house. I wanted to follow him – but something told me that was a bad idea. I merely watched as he disappeared around the front of the house. Thankfully, Steve's attention was still fixed on Derrick.

"If you don't want anyone to get hurt, then you'll leave," Steve growled.

"Just let us get her clothes," Derrick suggested.

"No."

I focused my gaze on Steve's brother, who was still standing inside the kitchen – on the other side of the open door. I saw his attention turn to something inside of the house, and he walked away from the door. Eliot.

Derrick must have realized what was going on, too, because he was determined to keep Steve's attention on him. He took five steps forward, moving in front of his mom and my mom, and squaring himself in front of Steve. Steve wasn't a big guy, but Derrick is fairly miniscule for a man. He's only 5'5" tall – and Steve had almost six inches on him.

"Steve, let's not make this an ugly scene."

"It's too late for that," Steve scoffed. He turned to see if his brother was still standing behind him. The look of shock that washed over his face when he saw Eliot step into the doorway would have been comical in any other situation. "How did you get in my house? Where are my brothers?"

"They're taking a nap," Eliot said smoothly. God, he's so hot.

Steve made a move to attack Eliot, but Eliot didn't look worried. He easily sidestepped him, grabbing Steve's arm and twisting it behind his back. "Settle down, Otis," he admonished.

Steve cried out in pain, trying to twist out of Eliot's iron grip. It was a fruitless fight. Derrick moved forward to Eliot's side. "You didn't kill anyone, did you?"

"No. They're all sitting in the living room."

"Sitting?"

"You'd be surprised how quickly some people will just do what they're told," Eliot countered.

After taking in the scene in front of us for a full minute, my mom turned to me. "He's handy to have around."

She turned back to Eliot and flashed him the first warm smile I'd seen her direct his way since she'd met him.

"I told you they would like me," Eliot smiled in my direction.

"They still don't like your hair," I shot back.

"You leave that boy alone," my mom admonished me. "His hair is beautiful. You should learn to be less judgmental."

What the hell?

Ten

Surprisingly, things went fairly smoothly after Eliot managed to defuse the situation with the mere threat of violence – and his really large biceps. He didn't actually say he would hurt them, but I noticed that Steve's brothers were watching him warily from their spot on the couch for the rest of the afternoon. I doubted he sweet talked them, but he was silent on whatever motivation he had provided for their sudden compromising behavior.

It didn't take too long to load Sally's stuff in the van – although moving furniture through the restaurant did prove troublesome when Eliot and Derrick started arguing about the best way to navigate the narrow hallway that led upstairs.

After a solid four hours of work, though, the job was complete and Eliot and I were on our way back to the city. The ride was actually fairly quiet – especially given the afternoon's excitement. Finally, I couldn't take it anymore.

"Well, my mom likes you now."

"Does that make me less attractive to you?"

"Why would you ask that?"

"I get the feeling that you get off on driving your mom crazy. If she likes me, that's one less thing you can needle her with."

He had a point.

"You're still attractive," I assured him. "I just wish you would have taken your shirt off so she could see your tattoos."

"Next time," Eliot promised.

I hadn't brought up the fact that he'd referred to himself as my boyfriend. I figured it wasn't necessary. I wasn't exactly looking to date anyone else – and he seemed relatively content with the fact that I wasn't boring. That was good enough for me right now.

When we got to my house, I was surprised to see a lone figure sitting on the front porch. As we pulled into the driveway, I could make out the small frame of my cousin, Lexie.

"Guess she's out of rehab," Eliot grimaced.

"Don't give her a hard time," I warned him.

"Fine," he said shortly.

We exited his truck and I walked over to Lexie. She was standing by the time I got to her. "Did they let you out, or are there people in uniforms looking for you because you escaped?"

I was going for levity, but it actually turned out to be a more serious question than I initially envisioned.

"I completed my full thirty days," Lexie said dismissively. She didn't look very happy for a woman that had just finished an important milestone in her life.

"How do you feel?" I asked cautiously.

"Fine," she said noncommittally. A worrisome thought rushed through my mind. I had a feeling that Lexie's sudden sobriety wasn't going to be long lived – especially if I couldn't get her focused on something else pretty quickly.

"What are you doing here?" Eliot asked.

"I need a place to stay," Lexie answered shortly. "Can I sleep on your couch until I find a place?"

"Sure," I answered. I never could say no to her. At least if she was staying here I'd be able to control some of what she did. Crap, that is something my mom would think.

I heard Eliot clear his throat beside me. Thankfully, he didn't say anything. He just gave me a worried glance instead.

"Are you dating him now?" Lexie gestured to Eliot as she slipped a strand of her brown hair behind her ear. It had gotten longer. In fact, it looked like she needed a good trim.

"Yes," I said truthfully.

At 4'11" tall, Lexie was slight. She glanced up at Eliot's face and regarded him for a moment. "If you don't want me to stay here, I won't."

"Why do you say that?"

"You're obviously having sex. I don't want to crimp your style."

"How am I obviously having sex?"

"You look a lot more relaxed than the last time I saw you," Lexie said simply.

"The last time you saw me we were almost blown up because one of your friends brought a nitrous tank to a gun fight," I reminded her.

"And I was shot," Eliot added.

I gave him a sidelong look. He really wasn't helping matters. He must have sensed that, so he took a step back. "I guess I'll leave you two to catch up," he said finally. He didn't look thrilled with the prospect.

"That's probably a good idea," I said.

I followed him over to his truck. Things were suddenly awkward. "Thanks for all your help," I said lamely.

Eliot smirked. He kissed me quickly, wrapping his arms around me for a second and then pulling away. "I'll call you tomorrow," he said. He climbed into his truck and then turned back to me. "If something happens, call me right away."

"What do you think is going to happen?"

"With her around? Anything is possible."

"We'll be fine," I promised him. I actually didn't know what he was so worried about. The odds of something exploding again were relatively long – especially since the last incident was barely a month old.

I led Lexie into the house. She was unusually quiet – even for her. When we got inside, she helped herself to a pop in the refrigerator and plopped down on the couch with a dramatic sigh.

"What's wrong?"

"What isn't wrong?"

I waited for her to continue. The whole family is dramatic, but Lexie could win an Academy Award.

"I have no serious boyfriend. No job. No prospects of any kind. I have a GED. My mom acts like she's proud I went to rehab, but I know she's really disappointed in the whole thing. Derrick won't even talk to me. And now I'm sleeping on your couch and infringing on the only sex you've had in years."

"It won't be forever," I prodded, ignoring her sex comment. Actually, I figured three weeks would be my absolute limit. "What do you want to do?"

"I want to be a soap opera actress, but I don't think that's going to happen," she said bitterly.

I could see her point. "Why don't you aim lower – just to start."

"Like what?"

"I was at Starbucks the other day and they're looking for a barista." She had worked for Starbucks several times over the past few years. I figured she probably wouldn't have a hard time getting rehired.

"Yeah," she sighed. "That's probably a good idea." She didn't sound too thrilled at the prospect. I didn't blame her.

"Just do it until you get back on your feet. Then we'll think of something else."

Lexie nodded and stared at the television as I flipped it on and turned it to Soap Net. We both love *General Hospital*. There is nothing a good dose of Luke, Laura and their extravagant adventures can't fix.

"I'm glad Genie Francis came back," Lexie said finally. "The show hasn't been the same without her."

"Me, too."

We lapsed into silence a few minutes. I could tell Lexie was mulling something over in her mind. I could only hope it was something reasonable, and not like the time when she decided that she wanted to run away from home and join the circus because she thought she could be freak on the sideshow circuit because she was so short.

"I've always wanted to teach yoga," she said finally.

"Have you ever taken a yoga class?"

"What does that have to do with anything?" She looked incredulous.

"I just think you have to actually know the right positions to be able to teach them," I said calmly.

"So, I'll take a class."

"I think you have to be a certified instructor to be able to teach," I said. Talking to Lexie is like talking to a toddler, I swear.

"How hard can it be to become a certified instructor?"

I had no idea. Lexie had the attention span of a gnat, though, so I doubted she would be able to complete even the basic courses – let alone the advanced. Plus, it's not exactly like anyone in our family can be called overtly athletic. Watching *The Biggest Loser* is usually enough of a workout for me.

"Why don't you get a job at Starbucks, take a class and then see how that goes?"

"Of course," Lexie scoffed. "I'm not an idiot."

Lexie and I spent the rest of the afternoon watching television and talking about rehab. She said it actually wasn't that bad after the first week. "Once I went through detox it was fine," she said.

"What did you do all day?" My only knowledge of rehab came from what I'd seen in television and movies. I wasn't sure how true it really was.

"It wasn't a state run hole, so it was actually pretty nice," Lexie said. "We had classes inside in the morning and afternoon meditation outside. We were close to the lake, so it was really pretty there."

That didn't sound like the Lexie I knew and loved.

"Plus, there were a lot of hot guys there," Lexie amended.

That sounded like the Lexie I had grown up with.

"I met one really cool guy," she continued. "His name is Raymond. He is really hot."

Lexie had spent the fast five years dating black guys. I figured rehab hadn't changed her sexual proclivities. "Is he black?"

"Why does that matter? You're really racist, you know."

"I'm not racist," I protested. "The last white guy you dated was in high school." She'd went through a Hispanic phase when she was living in Florida for two years after high school. Since then, though, she not only dated black men, but she actually thought she was black at certain times.

"He's not black. He's Dominican."

"How long is he in rehab?"

"Another two weeks. When he gets out, we're going to get a place together. I'm supposed to start looking."

"You barely know him," I started to argue. I bit my lower lip. I didn't really know why I was arguing with her. Lexie was proficient at the school of hard knocks. She had to learn every lesson the hard way. Plus, if she stuck to her schedule, that would mean she would be out of my house in two weeks. What? I'm not selfish. I really want what's best for her – and me.

"Sometimes you just know when you meet your soul mate," Lexie said.

Whatever. I decided to change tactics.

"Where are you going to look for a place at?"

"The city," Lexie said simply. "I can't stand living in the suburbs."

"So, let me get this straight," I said. "You're going to get a job at Starbucks, learn to be a yoga instructor, move to Detroit with a guy you just met in rehab and live happily ever after?"

"Pretty much."

That sounded like a marvelous idea.

Eleven

Lexie and I managed to refrain from heavy discussions for the rest of the night. I think that was a welcome development for both of us – since we weren't necessarily on the same wavelength as far as her job prospects went.

When I excused myself to retire for the night, I noticed that my cell phone was ringing. I recognized Eliot's phone number and picked it up immediately.

"How are things going?"

"They're fine," I lied.

"Really? Are they really fine or do you just not want to tell me I was right?"

Both. "They're really fine."

"What's her plan?"

Don't answer that. "She's going to look for a job at Starbucks Monday."

"Is she qualified to work there?"

"She's worked there before," I replied.

Eliot was quiet for a minute. "Did you lock up your valuables before you went to sleep?"

"You need to learn to lay off her," I admonished him. "She's nowhere near as bad as you seem to think?"

Eliot apparently didn't want to start a fight, so he changed the subject. "What are you doing tomorrow?"

"We're getting up early and going to breakfast," I said. "Then I have no idea what we're doing the rest of the afternoon. Why?"

"What's your idea of early?"

"I don't know, 11 a.m."

"You know that's actually the middle of the afternoon for some people," Eliot chuckled.

"Not anyone I hang around with."

Eliot ignored me. "You want to have dinner tomorrow and see a movie? We both have to be up early Monday morning, so I was thinking we could see like a 3 p.m. movie and then go to dinner."

"That sounds good to me," I started. Then I remembered Lexie. "What about Lexie?"

"What about her?"

"What is she going to do?"

"Polish her people skills?"

"You're not funny."

"I wasn't trying to be," Eliot challenged.

"I don't want to abandon her." Of course, for all I knew she had plans to visit her new boyfriend. I opened my bedroom door and called out to Lexie. "What are you doing tomorrow?"

"You mean after breakfast?"

"Yeah."

"I'm going back out to the rehab."

"You're going to see your new boyfriend?"

"Yeah."

"You'll be out there all afternoon?"

"Yeah."

I went back into the bedroom and shut the door. "Dinner and a movie will be fine. She's going to visit her boyfriend back at rehab."

The incredulous silence on the other end of the phone stretched into what felt like infinity. Finally, Eliot broke it. "She picked up a guy in rehab?"

"Yeah." I don't know why he was so surprised.

"He must be a real winner."

"I picked up you in a pawnshop," I pointed out.

"First off, I picked you up," Eliot corrected me. "Second off, I happen to own that pawnshop."

I didn't want to point out that his clarification wouldn't exactly work for everyone, but I didn't feel like now was the right time. "The good news is that she will be out of here in two weeks," I said brightly.

"What's the bad news? Wait . . . I'm not sure I want to know."

He definitely didn't want to know. "She's moving in with this new guy. They're soul mates."

"Nope. I didn't want to know."

The next morning – well, mid-morning – Lexie and I went to downtown Mount Clemens for breakfast. I didn't particularly care where we went – but Lexie wanted a good old fashioned Coney Island breakfast, so I took her to the best one in the area.

We both ordered eggs and hash browns. I had tomato juice, while Lexie had coffee. We shared a copy of The Monitor, with me perusing the news section and her looking through the classified ads. After a leisurely breakfast, we both got up to leave. Lexie grabbed my wrist and twisted it hard. "Don't turn around," she whispered.

I was momentarily confused. "Why?"

"Just trust me."

"How am I going to leave the building if I don't turn around?"

Lexie bit her lip. "Okay, turn around. Try not to scream, though."

I slowly turned around. I don't know what I was expecting. A naked guy with a hangover, perhaps, or maybe a guy dressed up like a clown. What I saw, though, was something completely different. Jake was entering the building. He was dressed casually for the day – obviously he wasn't working – and he wasn't alone.

A tall and willowy blonde followed him into the building and they were chatting amiably. He hadn't seen me yet.

"Do you want to crawl under the table?" Lexie offered helpfully.

"No," I scoffed. I considered it silently for a second. No, that will never work. He'd eventually see me.

"What do you want to do?" Lexie's eyes were so big I thought they were going to pop out of her head. She was panicking. I had no idea why. All I knew is that now that she was panicking, I was starting to panic, too. What a mess.

"We're not going to do anything," I cautioned her. "If he notices us, fine, we'll say hi and go on our way."

"And if he doesn't notice us?"

"Then I'll know I've suddenly been imbued with that super power I always wanted," I mumbled.

"I thought you wanted to be able to turn into the *Incredible Hulk*?" That would be cool.

"Just, let's go," I grabbed her wrist and started to lead her out of the restaurant. Unfortunately, I'd inadvertently grabbed her arm so hard she yelped in pain. All eyes in the restaurant swiveled to us – including Jake's. Crap.

Jake smirked when he saw us. "Avery," he greeted me stiffly. He was clearly amused by our antics, but still mad from the previous case we had all been involved in together.

"Jake," I smiled back at him. I could only hope the smile looked genuine and not deranged.

"Lexie." The tone of Jake's voice dropped a decibel. He sounded even more disappointed to see her than me. That was at least something.

"Hey, Jake," Lexie said smoothly. "How are things?"

"How are things with you?" He raised an eyebrow and regarded her speculatively.

"You know, I just got out of rehab."

"How did that go?"

Lexie shrugged. I could tell she was nervous. Still, she was trying to hold it together for me at this point. "You know shaking, vomiting, meditating – the usual."

"Sounds like you learned a lot," Jake said, motioning for his super model date to take a seat in the booth across the aisle from us. She hadn't spoken yet – which I was profoundly grateful for. "Hopefully it will stick," he admonished Lexie.

"Oh, I'm sure it will," Lexie twiddled her thumbs nervously. "I'm staying at Avery's for the next two weeks – and she won't let me fall off the wagon." I think Lexie meant for that to be encouraging. Jake grimaced when he heard it, though.

"She's staying with you?"

"Yes." The word came out in an uncomfortable squeak.

"Do you think that's a good idea?"

"Why not?"

"You know why," he said. "Why don't you stay in the apartment above the restaurant?" He turned to Lexie.

"Sally is staying there."

"Why is Sally staying there?" Jake had grown up in close proximity to my family. He knew who all the players were.

"She left Steve," Lexie said.

"Why?"

"He's a dick."

"Hasn't he always been a dick?"

"Pretty much."

Watching Lexie and Jake converse, felt like I was in a weird episode of the Twilight Zone for a second. Their distraction with each other allowed Jake's girlfriend and me to size each other up. I didn't get the feeling that she felt all that intimidated.

"So Sally left Steve? Why don't you go home and move in with your mom?" Jake suggested. What was his deal? Why did he even care?

"I'm only staying with Avery for two weeks," Lexie pointed out. "I have a new boyfriend and when he gets out of rehab we're moving in together."

"You met a boyfriend in rehab?" I could tell Jake wasn't exactly impressed by that fact.

"Yeah. We want to get our own place in the city. And, besides, with Avery sleeping with Eliot now, I don't think she wants me around that long." As soon as she said the words, Lexie realized her mistake. She shot me an apologetic look.

I was frozen in fear – well, not exactly fear, but shock. I knew Jake would have to find out eventually, but I couldn't imagine a worse time for him to hear the news.

I saw the muscle in Jake's cheek work for a second. Then he fixed a set glare on me. "You and Kane are officially an item now, huh?"

I thought about lying. I figured that was the wrong move, though. Not only would the truth eventually come out, but if the fact that I lied about our relationship ever made it back to Eliot he would be hurt – and I didn't want that. I decided to do something I wasn't accustomed to: tell the truth. "We are." I squared my shoulders and waited for the diatribe about how dangerous Eliot was to rain down on me. It never came, though.

"I'm happy for you," Jake said stiffly. I could tell he wasn't really happy. Still, he was trying not to unload on me – so that was at least something.

"Thanks," I mumbled.

"This is Shelly," he finally introduced the woman at his side. For her part, she had watched the exchange with a mixture of curiosity and rampant jealousy. I knew the feeling.

Since Jake was being such an adult, though, I decided I should probably try to do the same. I extended my hand to Shelly and introduced myself. "I'm Avery."

"You're the reporter for The Monitor?" I could tell Shelly wasn't completely up to speed on my past with Jake. I figured that it wasn't exactly my job to tell her.

"I am," I said.

"The one that stole evidence from a crime scene?"

I shot a dark look in Jake's direction. So much for being adults. "I didn't steal evidence," I corrected her. "I borrowed a flash drive and I forgot I had it."

"That's called stealing," Jake challenged me.

"No it's not," I shot back.

"Yes it is!" Jake's face was starting to get red. He was going to pop a gasket.

"I guess we'll just have to agree to disagree," I huffed.

"I guess so."

Jake and I stared each other down for a few minutes. Finally, Lexie stepped in and started to pull me away. "We should be going," she said apologetically.

I let Lexie pull me out of the building, but not before I shot one last dark glare back in Jake's direction. "He has a lot of nerve," I grumbled.

Just before the door swung shut behind us, I heard Shelly's melodic voice waft through the open space. "It was nice to meet you."

I made a move to charge back through the doors but Lexie stopped me. "It's not worth it."

"She did that on purpose," I challenged.

"Oh, she's a total whore," Lexie agreed. "But if you go back in there things are going to get ugly."

"They're already ugly."

"Uglier," Lexie corrected herself.

"Great," I growled.

"Look at it this way, at least you don't have to tell him about Eliot now."

Thank the world for small favors.

Twelve

The next day I woke up with what felt like a raging hangover. Since I hadn't had anything alcoholic to drink, I blamed Jake. It was just like him to purposely give me a migraine.

I had gone to dinner with Eliot last night, but I hadn't told him about my run-in with Jake. Until I figured out how I felt about the situation, I couldn't put into words what had happened. If he asked, I would tell him that I told Jake about us. I wouldn't give him all the gritty details, though. I didn't figure anyone needed to know those. I was there, and even I didn't want to know.

I left Lexie still asleep. She had promised she would look for a job in the afternoon. I figured that was a 50-50 proposition at best.

Instead of going into the office, I headed straight out to the Frank house in Romeo. Fish had texted me the night before and told me that I should check in with Brian Frank and do a follow-up on his missing wife. I think Fish was anticipating – like I was – that the story would turn into more in the future.

When I got out to the Frank house, I wasn't surprised to see more media than the first time. Two of the four local television stations were there, and both the big Detroit dailies. This was in addition to representatives from three local weeklies and another smaller daily from St. Clair County. Media can smell blood in the water. We're like sharks that way. I think everyone was holding their breath and waiting for this thing to explode into a media frenzy.

When I got out of the car, I was surprised to see Eliot's truck parked up the street. What was he doing here?

I looked around to see if I could find him, but I didn't see him anywhere. I stepped up to the media throng. "Where's everyone at?" I asked.

"They're not out yet," said the Channel 2 reporter I had fought with the other day answered dismissively.

Devon Lange, the Channel 4 reporter, turned to me with a bright smile. "Avery," she greeted me with false excitement.

"Devon," I nodded. We pretended we didn't loathe each other on sight — mostly for Derrick's sake. I could only hope he would be able to see through her façade sooner — rather than later — and I would never have to see her again. Okay, that was wishful thinking. Still, the longer he dated her the more she irritated me. I was convinced that was the only reason he kept dating her.

I noticed Tony Winters walk out of the Frank house and head our way. I was glad that he was still in charge of the investigation. After my uncomfortable run-in with Jake yesterday, I wasn't exactly looking forward to seeing him again.

"Is he on his way out?" I asked Tony.

"Yeah," Tony said. "He's just finishing something up."

"Are we expecting any big developments today?" I asked him.

"No," Tony feigned surprise. "Should we be?" If I wasn't convinced before that law enforcement was hiding something from me, I would be now. I don't know who they think they're messing with.

When Tony sauntered over to chat with the Detroit daily representatives, I felt Devon at my elbow. "What do you think they're hiding?" She asked.

I was surprised. I didn't think she had the brain matter to catch on to the fact that something else was going on. "I have no idea. Whatever it is, though, I think it's big."

"Yeah. I think they think she's dead," Devon said.

"Me, too," I admitted. "I think they think it's the husband – but they can't prove it."

"Of course they think it's the husband. Law enforcement always thinks it's the husband," she scoffed. I couldn't help but wonder if she'd shared her disdain for law enforcement lethargy to Derrick. Despite myself, though, I liked her a smidgen more than I had before.

"Who do you think did it?"

"Oh, it's definitely the husband," Devon answered. "Have you seen his eyes? No innocent person has eyes like that."

What? That's a totally reasonable assumption.

"How do you think he did it?" Devon mulled over the question. We were starting to draw interest from the other reporters, and they were closing in on us.

"I think he probably shot her," Devon finally said.

"There's no gun registered in his name," one of the weekly writers supplied. "I did a background check."

"That doesn't mean he doesn't own a gun," Devon laughed. "Just that he doesn't legally own a handgun."

She had a point.

"I think he strangled her," one of the Detroit daily reporters answered. "He looks like a guy that would strangle someone."

He did look like a guy that would strangle someone.

Devon turned to me expectantly. I had no idea how she had died. Still, I felt pressured to offer some sort of answer – even if I wasn't serious. "I think he chopped her into bits and hid her in one of the parks," I finally said.

The Channel 2 reporter, Ariel Cook, gave me a dirty look. "You shouldn't be joking about stuff like this. This is a wife and mother here. You guys shouldn't be acting like assholes. You make us all look bad."

Devon and I shared a mutinous grimace. She'd learn. And, if nothing else, a common enemy was now bringing us closer together. I couldn't help but wonder – for a second at least – if this would make Derrick happy or completely infuriate him.

I didn't get a chance to dwell on the question that long. The front door to the Frank house had swung open again and Brian Frank was now heading in our direction. He looked even more disheveled than he had a few days ago. If I had to guess, he hadn't showered (or shaved) in that entire time. It didn't look like he was getting more than a few hours of sleep a night either – at least if his red-rimmed eyes were any indication.

While Brian Frank's appearance was jarring, my eyes fixed on the figure at his side as he exited his house. It was a familiar figure: Eliot. He met my gaze as he crossed the lawn. His expression was hard to read. Mine was grim. What the hell was he doing here?

Brian Frank greeted everyone like we were old acquaintances. He even tried to move in for a hug a couple of times – only with women, go figure – but most sidestepped him. That wasn't how we were used to doing business.

He started the press conference by saying that hundreds of leads had been called in to the sheriff's department – including sightings in other countries – and he was hopeful that Sarah would be found relatively soon.

I tried to gauge Tony's reaction to Brian's comments – but Tony barely moved. Brian also announced that thanks to his wife's company, an accounting firm in Detroit, he was able to offer a $25,000 reward for information that led to her safe return.

After repeating – almost verbatim – his pleas that his wife come home, Brian Frank turned over the news conference for questions.

"Who's your hot friend," Ariel asked, smiling flirtatiously in Eliot's direction.

"This is Eliot Kane," Brian introduced Eliot. "He's a local investigator and I've hired him to try and help me track down leads."

Investigator? I regarded Eliot solemnly for a second. I didn't question his credentials, though.

"That's probably pretty smart," Ariel said sagely. "If he's a professional, he'll know better places to look."

Brian Frank shot Ariel a grateful look. "Thanks. That's what I thought, too."

Oh, gag me.

After a few more questions, Brian ended the press conference. He reminded everyone that he was available on his own personal cell phone should we have more questions. I sidled over to Tony when I was sure no one was looking and regarded him seriously for a moment. "Where are you guys looking for her?"

Tony met my gaze evenly. I could tell I was making him nervous. "We're not looking anywhere specific, Ms. Shaw," he stressed my name. "We're asking for the public's help. She's out there somewhere. Someone knows where she is. We just need people to call in tips."

Right.

I watched as Ariel scooted in closer to Eliot. She put her hand on his arm to get his attention. "Mr. Kane, I would love to get your thoughts on how the investigation should proceed," I heard her giggle breathlessly. "Maybe we could talk about that over lunch."

I saw Eliot's gaze lift and meet mine. I could see a smile playing at the corner of his lips. "I'm not here to talk to the press, Miss . . . " I couldn't help but smirk to myself that Eliot had no idea who she was.

"Call me Ariel," she interjected. "Like *The Little Mermaid*."

"Ariel," Eliot looked uncomfortable. "I won't be doing any press."

I saw Eliot's gaze shoot to me again. I could feel my cheeks starting to color.

"Doesn't look that way to me," Tony scoffed.

"What?"

"Nothing," Tony said with a false innocent air. "I was just commenting on how it looks like he's doing at least one member of the press."

I gave Tony a dirty look. "Who told you that?"

"The two of you just did," he laughed. "I'm a trained investigator – and you two aren't doing a very good job of hiding your feelings."

I fixed Tony with my best PMS look. "Okay," he conceded. "Derrick might have mentioned it."

I knew it!

"And Jake might have mentioned something about it yesterday at the gun range."

Uh-oh.

"You went to the gun range with Jake?"

"Yeah. He was in a bad mood. That's where we always go when he's in a bad mood."

"Why was he in a bad mood?" I asked cautiously.

"I don't know," Tony shrugged.

My rampant narcissistic streak was hoping he was jealous of me and Eliot. My practical side figured it was probably something more. I decided to change the subject. "Is Eliot a licensed private investigator?"

"Isn't that something you should ask him?"

"I guess," I said finally. "It just didn't occur to me."

"He's been involved in quite a few cases," Tony said.

Eliot was still trying to extricate himself from Ariel, I noticed. Maybe I should go save him? Instead, I was surprised to see Brian Frank step in front of me.

"Ms. Shaw," he said, extending his hand in greeting. I took it warily. "I just wanted to thank you personally for coming out here."

"It's my job," I said simply.

"I know. It's just that you've got a sterling reputation and I'm so glad that a reporter of your caliber is on my wife's case."

I couldn't tell if he was making fun of me or not. The fact that Tony was shaking with silent laughter beside me didn't fill me with a lot of hope that he was being sincere.

"Well, thank you," I said finally.

I noticed Eliot making his way over to the two of us. He was regarding Brian Frank somewhat warily. "Mr. Kane, this is Avery Shaw. She's a reporter for The Monitor."

"I know Ms. Shaw," Eliot said finally.

"You do?" Brian seemed surprised.

"We've crossed paths before," Eliot said briefly.

"I bet," Tony snickered under his breath. I shot him a dirty look.

Brian Frank seemed oblivious. "I was just telling her how happy we are to have her on the case."

Eliot nodded, but he didn't say anything. I was starting to feel decidedly uncomfortable, so I excused myself. "I have to go back to the office and write my story," I explained.

"Of course," Brian said. "It's such a glamorous job."

I shook my head briefly and started to move away. I saw Eliot mime a telephone near his head. I nodded and kept moving away. His message was clear; he would call and explain as soon as he could get away from Brian Frank.

I couldn't wait for the explanation.

As I started to move away, my own cell phone started to ring. I answered it without looking to see who was calling. I was stunned when I realized who was on the other end of the line.

"Hey, Jake," I said warily.

I saw Eliot stiffen next to Brian Frank out of the corner of my eye.

"I need to talk to you," Jake said.

"About what?"

"The Frank case," he said briefly.

"Okay," I said warily.

"Can you meet me for lunch?"

"I guess I can do that," I said reluctantly.

"You want to go to the Coney?" If Jake was aware of my uncomfortable situation right now, he didn't let on. Of course, if I had to guess, he wouldn't care either way. Bothering Eliot would just be a bonus in his book right now.

"That's fine," I sighed.

"Good. See you in a half an hour?"

I glanced at Eliot, who was still staring at me with a grave look on his face.

"Better make it forty-five minutes," I said.

Thirteen

I could tell Eliot wanted to question me about my call from Jake – but he also didn't want to cause a scene in front of his new client. He settled for standing at Brian Frank's side and casting me speculative looks from a few feet away.

Tony Winters wasn't as subtle. "What did Jake want?"

I felt a sudden urge to smack Tony – or gag him. "He said he had something specific he wanted to talk to me about regarding the case," I said carefully, glancing up at Eliot briefly. He didn't look happy.

Tony was as oblivious as ever. "That's weird. Why would he want to give you special information?"

Maybe because he wanted to talk about our ridiculously uncomfortable run-in yesterday. "I have no idea."

I said my goodbyes to everyone, exchanging one last furtive look with Eliot, and then headed off to my meeting lunch with Jake. During the half hour drive, I couldn't help but run crazy scenarios of what was about to happen through my head.

In one, Jake announced he had fallen in love with Shelly at first sight and they were getting married because she was pregnant. Unlikely, I know.

In the second, Jake announced he had dumped Shelly right after he saw me because he couldn't live without me anymore. Even more unlikely.

In the third, Eliot raced into the Coney and he and Jake fought to the death to see whom I would end up with. You can see why

I shouldn't be left with my own thoughts very often. My mind is a dangerous – and preposterous – place.

By the time I reached the Coney, I had worked myself into a nervous little ball of energy. This wouldn't be good.

I stopped outside the door long enough to catch my breath. Then I squared my shoulders, caught my reflection in the glass of the door briefly, and entered the restaurant. I wasn't surprised to see Jake already sitting at a booth and sipping from a cup of coffee.

He looked up when he heard the door open. He didn't smile when he saw me. I guess he wasn't about to admit his undying love. I was so focused on Jake, I didn't notice when I stepped in front of a waitress – causing her to veer off to the left and drop the tray she was carrying with a loud clatter. Everyone in the restaurant turned in my direction.

"I'm so sorry," I bent down to try and help the waitress pick up the plates she had just scattered across the floor.

"You should watch where you're walking," she admonished me.

"I didn't see you," I offered lamely.

"I've got it," the waitress growled.

"Let me help."

She slapped my hand away anxiously. "I said I've got it."

I stood back up and turned back towards Jake. I could see he was doubled over the table and shaking with laughter. "It's not funny," I grumbled as I slid into the booth across from him.

"It's pretty funny," he sputtered.

Whatever.

A different waitress made her way over to the table. She slid a glance over to her co-worker, who was muttering under her breath as she continued to clean up the dishes, and then turned back to us. "Do you know what you want?"

"I'll have two Coneys, an order of chili fries and a large diet pop," I said.

Jake raised an eyebrow as he regarded me. "Quite a refined palate you've got there," he said. "I especially like how you ordered 2,000 calories of food and then finished it off with a diet pop."

"I don't want to get fat," I shrugged.

Jake smirked. The tension was obviously broken – for the time being, at least.

I watched as he ordered a Greek salad – with dressing on the side – and then waited until the waitress had walked away. He then turned his attention to me. "I'm glad you agreed to come," he said finally.

"Why wouldn't I?" That was a loaded question, I know.

"Yesterday," Jake said simply.

I decided to play dumb. "What happened yesterday?"

Jake shook his head. "Don't do that. I don't have time to sit here and watch you play games."

"I don't know what you mean," I sniffed.

"Avery, let's not do this. Let's pretend we're adults."

Pretend being the operative word.

"Fine. What about yesterday?"

"I want to apologize for introducing Shelly to you that way."

"You don't owe me anything," I reminded him.

"I know I don't. It's just that . . . I don't know . . . our lives are so intertwined. The whole situation was surreal. Especially with Lexie there."

"Lexie never helps any situation," I reminded him. "You've been around her long enough to know that."

Jake ran his hands through his hair in frustration. "I know. It was just such a ridiculous situation."

No more ridiculous than any other situation in my life.

"Shelly seems nice," I said finally.

"She is," Jake nodded.

"How long have you been dating?"

"About six weeks."

Wait, what? I ran the math through my head. That didn't quite add up. "You were dating her during that whole Oxy trade scandal?"

Jake met my gaze evenly. "I had just started."

I wracked my brain. If that were true, why did I remember him flirting with me? What an ass. "Well . . . good for you," I forced out.

"I didn't know, back then, if it was going anywhere," Jake clarified.

"You don't owe me any explanations," I repeated. "It's really none of my business."

Jake watched my face. I don't know what he was looking for, and quite frankly I was so infuriated I didn't care. I had been dreading telling him about Eliot, feeling guilty about it, and he had been lying for weeks. I felt like such an idiot.

"You sound angry," he said.

"I'm not angry," I lied.

"You sound angry," he repeated.

"I'm not angry."

"Well . . . you sound angry."

"I'm not angry!" My voice was starting to carry across the restaurant.

"Fine, you're not angry," Jake acquiesced.

We sat in silent for a few minutes. Thankfully, the waitress picked now to deliver our food. I dug into the greasy goodness and steadfastly tried to pretend that Jake wasn't staring at me from across the table. After eating in silence for a few minutes, Jake couldn't take the uncomfortable vibe emanating from the table. For my part, I had chosen to ignore it.

"I don't see why you're so angry," Jake started.

"Don't start that again," I growled.

"Seriously. You've been dating Kane for weeks, and yet you're angry at me?"

"I have not been dating him for weeks," I scoffed.

Jake looked surprised. "What do you mean?"

"We've only been dating for a couple of days," I corrected him. "Our first official date was Friday."

Jake took in the new information and mulled it for a minute. "I thought you had been dating since he got shot," he admitted.

"Why would that possibly matter? You've been dating Shelly since before that time." For the life of me, I couldn't explain why this was bothering me so much. It's not like I didn't know Jake dated – it's the fact that he had hidden it from me for so long that was driving me insane.

"I know but . . . if I had known . . . I," Jake was stumbling over his words.

I couldn't take it anymore. This conversation wasn't going to get us anywhere, and I was done trying to pretend that I wasn't completely irritated with him. "It doesn't matter now. What did you want to talk about regarding the Frank case?" I was suddenly all business.

Jake noticed the shift in my attitude. If he wanted to challenge it, he obviously thought better of it. "I know you've been asking Tony some pointed questions," he finally said.

"Define pointed."

"You keep insinuating that we're hiding information from you," Jake said.

"You are."

Jake shot me a dark look. "Why do you say that?"

"I'm not new, Jake. I know it's weird for the sheriff's department to hold press conferences on a missing woman at the home of that missing woman – and in conjunction with her husband."

"Just because we haven't done it before, that doesn't mean it's weird," Jake argued vehemently.

"Right," I said sarcastically. "Jake, you know I'm not going to believe that – no matter how you try to dress it up – so I have to wonder what your real purpose in calling me here was?"

"I just want to tell you that you're barking up the wrong tree," Jake said, shifting his gaze to the left as he said the words. That's a sign of lying. I knew it!

"I think you're worried I'm going to ruin whatever little operation you've got going on," I countered.

"I think you're paranoid," Jake shot back. "I think you've got some little conspiracy theory running around your overactive imagination."

"Say you're right, why do you care?"

Jake looked blank. "What do you mean?"

"If it's all in my head, what are you worried about?"

I had clearly hit a nerve, because Jake shifted uncomfortably. "I think you're missing the point."

"No, I'm not," I said triumphantly. "You think she's dead and he did it and you're letting him hold press conferences out at the house because it gives you access to the house without naming him as a suspect."

"That's . . . that's just ridiculous," Jake sputtered.

"I'm right. I know it."

"You haven't told anyone else your theory, have you?" Jake looked perplexed.

I shook my head and smiled to myself. "No, I haven't, Jake. I'm not in the habit of sharing my news gathering skills with others."

"Skills?"

Luck, skills, whatever.

"I knew I was on the right track. Tony is a terrible liar." I was happily patting myself on the back for my superior deductive skills.

"I don't want you spreading this theory around," Jake warned me.

I met Jake's gaze evenly. I knew he was worried I was going to start investigating this story – and it would screw up what he was trying to do. "I won't spread my theory around," I reluctantly agreed.

"And maybe you should pass this story on to someone else at the paper," Jake prodded.

Yeah, that wasn't going to happen. "I'm not going to request a change in assignments."

"Try to be professional," Jake said.

"I'm always professional."

Jake glanced at my *Harold and Maude* shirt and then eyed me doubtfully.

"We both have a job to do, Jake," I said, ignoring his dubious wardrobe assessment. "Why don't we focus on our jobs and let things happen as they're going to happen and go from there?"

"Fine," Jake said shortly. He stood up from the table and tossed enough money to cover both of our meals on the table. "While we're doing our jobs, why don't you remind Kane that it's a crime to infringe a police investigation?"

Well, that answered the question about whether or not he knew that Brian Frank had hired Eliot.

"Why don't you tell him that?" I countered.

"I don't particularly want to spend any time with him," Jake said truthfully. They had a stressful relationship long before I had been caught between the two of them. Years ago they had been Army Rangers together – and something had happened that had driven a wedge between the two of them. I had no idea what that something was – but the curiosity was killing me. Neither one of them would tell me. "Just tell him that if he comes across something he thinks we should know, he's legally bound to tell us."

I had no idea if that was true, but I doubted Eliot would protect a murderer. "I'll tell him," I said finally.

"Good."

Jake turned to leave the restaurant, but he swung back suddenly. "Be careful," he warned me.

"Of what? Eliot?" Now I was confused.

"You should always be careful around Eliot," Jake said dismissively. "I meant that you should be careful when you're investigating this story. Things could get dangerous."

"Because Brian Frank is a murderer?" I was honestly curious what he would say.

"Because a woman is missing and we have no idea what happened to her," Jake replied. "As much of a pain in the ass as you are, and you're pretty much the biggest pain in the ass I've ever met, I would hate to think of something bad happening to you."

That was the nicest thing he had said to me in weeks.

Fourteen

After lunch, I went back to the office to write my story. I was still flustered by my lunch with Jake. I honestly didn't know how to feel about the whole situation – so I decided to handle it the only way I knew how: Ignore it.

When I got to the office I saw that Marvin was in the middle aisle of the cubicles, gesturing wildly.

"What happened?"

Marvin looked up when I entered. "I was just telling them about my date last night."

Marvin was far too excited. That always made me nervous. "What happened?" What? It makes me nervous, but it's like a train wreck, you can't not look.

"I took her dancing."

"And she laughed because you have no rhythm?"

"No, worse," Marvin said. "And I do too have rhythm."

Is negative rhythm a thing?

"So what happened?" I dropped my notebook and purse on my desk and turned to him to give him my full attention.

"Well, we went out for a nice dinner," Marvin began, rubbing his hands together. "She ordered surf and turf, so I knew I was going to get some."

"What does surf and turf have to do with sex?"

Marvin looked at me incredulously. "You don't order an expensive meal unless you're willing to reciprocate."

"So you're buying sex? Like she's a prostitute?"

Marvin glared at me. "Do you want to hear the story or not?"

"I'm sorry, continue. You bought her a sex meal and . . ."

"And afterwards, I wanted to go for a walk on the beach and she wanted to go dancing."

"What beach?"

"The one along the canal in the Shores."

"Isn't that filthy and dirty and polluted with PCBs?"

"She doesn't know that."

Of course.

"So, anyway," he continued. "I finally took her to this place down the road – the Boat Basin. It was supposed to be upscale. When we got there, though, they didn't even have any name-brand amaretto."

Marvin fancies himself a man's man – a consummate ladies man – and yet he drinks like a woman.

"So you started a scene?"

"I don't cause scenes," Marvin countered. "I just made my displeasure obvious."

"So you made an ass of yourself," I interjected.

Marvin pretended he hadn't heard me. "So, after having a few drinks, we went out to dance."

"What were you wearing?" I asked.

"What does that matter?"

"I'm just trying to paint a picture in my mind."

"I was wearing my good suit."

"The purple one?" Marvin's good suit was really a polyester nightmare that was an awful shade of eggplant. He's the only one that didn't seem to know that it was tacky.

"Yes." Marvin was starting to get annoyed with my constant interruptions, so I shut my mouth. "Anyway, we went out on the dance floor and I decided to get fancy."

Uh-oh.

"You know how the dancers on *Dancing With the Stars* twirl people around?"

I nodded, exchanging a quick look with another reporter. I could already tell where this story was going. It's sad to think I was underplaying it in my mind.

"So, it was going well at first," Marvin started reenacting his movements. "I was holding on to one of her hands and twirling her in towards me and then out towards the crowd. It was going well and she seemed to be having a good time. I guess I got a little overzealous, because I flipped her out a little too far and I lost my grip on her hand."

I couldn't mentally look.

"She kind of stumbled back and fell into the band," Marvin said sheepishly. "It made a really loud noise and they had all these amps stacked up and she fell into them and the one on the top toppled over onto the ground."

"Was everyone staring?" One of the other reporters asked the question, but I wanted to hear the answer.

"Yeah. The band stopped playing and everyone was looking at me so . . . I kind of panicked."

"What do you mean, you panicked?"

"Well, everyone was staring at me. I could have walked over to her and helped her up, but then I figured everyone would know I was with her."

Perish the thought.

"I looked around, and the door to leave was right across from me," Marvin bit his lower lip.

"You didn't?"

"I did. I just walked out the door."

"And you left her there on the ground?"

"Yeah."

"How did she get home?"

"I have no idea."

"You didn't even wait in the parking lot for her?" I was incredulous.

"No. I figured she would be mad."

"Well, she's definitely going to be mad now," I offered.

"Do you think I should call her?"

"What would you say?"

"Well, I did buy her dinner, maybe she's not too mad."

"Oh, she's mad," I countered. "Unless you want to be castrated in your sleep, I'd probably let this one go."

"I really thought she was the one," Marvin lamented.

I didn't tell him that most guys don't abandon "the one" on the dirty floor of a dance club. I didn't think it would be a productive argument. "Well, I'm sure there will be a new prospect relatively soon." There always was.

"Yeah, but now I can't go back to my favorite bar because she works there." That's what was really bothering him.

"Maybe you can get her fired," I joked.

Marvin looked like he was contemplating the suggestion. "I am a good customer there."

I left Marvin with his thoughts. I could only hope he wouldn't go that far – but I'd known him long enough to realize that he might actually do it. Instead, I made my way over to Fred Fish's desk to give him an update. I left out the part about Jake's warnings and my suspicions. I didn't think it was time to let Fish know I was getting ready to infuriate local law enforcement – again.

I saw movement out of the corner of my eye. I knew who it was before I even looked up. Duncan Marlow, aka the office tool. Great. He was the last person I wanted to talk to.

"I have the camera, Fred," he proudly announced.

"Good," Fish answered. He turned to me. "Duncan is going to be working on the Sarah Frank story with you from now on."

Like hell.

"I don't need help," I said hurriedly.

"I don't care what you think you need. We have a new point-of-view camera, and we're looking for a story to test it out on. We think this will be a good one."

Since newspapers are more about online than print these days, video had become a big deal lately. All the reporters at The Monitor were equipped with handheld cameras that we were supposed to use on every story. Most of us conveniently "forgot" them back at the office.

"What are we going to use a point-of-view camera for on a missing persons case?" I was trying to find a tactful way out of this. Fish was clearly still mad at me and was punishing me by making me spend time with Duncan. There could be no other explanation.

"I figured I could retrace her last steps with the point of view camera to give our readers a real feeling of what she went through," Duncan said.

"We don't know what her last steps were," I pointed out.

"Well, then maybe I can walk through the house with it."

"We haven't been in the house," I countered.

"Well, I'm sure we can use it for something."

"I don't know what." I was faking pragmatism, but I was internally seething. I was not spending time with Duncan if I could possibly help it.

"I'm sure you'll figure out something," Fish waved off my protestations.

The only thing I could even think of was that the point-of-view camera would catch the crime when I was forced to kill Duncan after spending more than five minutes with him.

"I don't want him with me constantly," I blurted out.

"It's not exactly a dream come true for me either," Duncan deadpanned.

I ignored him. "You know what he's like," I continued. "He'll alienate everyone on the case and we'll never get a good story."

"You'll be in charge of making sure he doesn't do anything stupid," Fish supplied.

"I'm not a miracle worker," I said. I noticed Duncan glaring daggers at both of us. I could feel another uncomfortable human resources meeting in my future. Duncan had them on speed dial – and I was one of his most frequent targets. No one was safe, though. A couple of weeks ago he had made an appointment with the publisher to complain that everyone in the office was disrespecting him. Of course, he didn't seem to realize that we all hated him because he was the type of guy that went to the publisher to complain that people were disrespecting him. It was a vicious little cycle.

"I have faith in you," Fish said. I saw the twinkle in his eye. I was right. He was doing this on purpose.

"I know what you're doing," I announced.

"I don't know what you mean," he said with faux innocence.

"Not only do I know what you're doing, you know I know what you're doing."

"What I'm doing is expecting you to put together an impressive package for the upcoming weekend – and I expect Duncan to have some sort of video to go along with it."

Duncan was regarding me with his smug little pinched face.

"Fine," I blew out a sigh. "I can't guarantee he'll survive the week, though," I warned.

"I know. Maybe that will be another bonus?"

Given the look on Duncan's face, I had a feeling Fish was going to be heading to the human resources department, too.

Fifteen

After I left work that afternoon, I was still fuming. I had to figure out a way to get out of teaming with Duncan. He was like herpes. I avoided him as much as possible, but when there was an outbreak it was painful and annoying – and really hard to get rid of.

I was in a sticky situation here. Fish was clearly testing me to see if my newfound dedication to my craft was going to stick. Of course, he could be punishing me for his own enjoyment, too. If I were him, I'd make me miserable on a regular basis. I'm massively annoying. I can admit it. I'm not oblivious to my shortcomings.

When I got to the house, I entered through the back door. I heard the television in the living room and figured Lexie's job hunt probably hadn't lasted very long this afternoon.

When I got to the dining room – which opens into the living room – I saw Lexie stretching herself like a pretzel in front of the television. "What are you doing? That looks like it hurts."

Lexie's face was red with effort. "It feels great," she huffed. I could tell she was lying. She had to be lying. There was no way that position was anything other than sheer torture.

"But what are you doing?"

"I'm practicing yoga."

I glanced at the television and saw that she was watching some exercise show and trying to mimic the moves. "How did the job hunt go?"

"I got hired at the Starbucks down the road," she said as she tried to maneuver herself into another position.

"And?"

"I start tomorrow."

"Well, that's good."

"I'm working the morning shift."

"So, why are you doing this?"

"I told you I wanted to be a yoga instructor. Did you forget?"

"No. I just figured you'd forget about it."

"Well, I didn't. I'm telling you, this is my passion."

I didn't think passion was meant to look like medieval torture, but I kept that thought to myself. "Did you visit Raymond at the rehab?"

"Yeah. He's excited. I told him how bendy I'm going to be by the time he gets out. He can't wait."

I bet.

"So what did you do all afternoon?"

"I got the job before noon, so I took the opportunity to go to a yoga class at that gym around the corner."

"That weird hippie one with all the green teas in the window?" I involuntarily shuddered.

"It's a place of calm and serenity. Not a hippie place with tea," Lexie corrected me caustically.

"The people that go there look stoned," I pointed out.

"They're high on life."

Life, reefer, whatever.

"Are you sure that's an environment you should be in?" I asked cautiously.

"I don't know what you're talking about," Lexie feigned ignorance.

"I thought the rehab place told you to stay out of places that would tempt you with, um, herbal supplements." I just want to point out, I'm not a pot hater. In fact, if I wasn't randomly drug tested I would probably partake from time to time myself. However, there's a difference between occasionally imbibing and spending your day baked on the couch watching *The Wiggles*. It was a distinction that was often wasted on Lexie.

"They're not potheads," she argued. "Yeah, sure, I think some of them smoke recreationally, but it's not like it's some big drug den."

Watching Lexie try to twist herself into a position that couldn't possibly be comfortable, I had my doubts. I figured you'd have to be high to even try that.

"Anyway," Lexie continued. "I went to a class and the only one they had was a hot yoga class, so I went to that."

I plopped down on the couch so I could continue to watch Lexie's endeavors and be comfortable at the same time. "I've heard about that. Isn't that where they turn up the heat to like 100 degrees and then try to sweat you until you die?"

"No. It's meant to help loosen your muscles, clear your airways and help you sweat out your toxins."

Lexie had obviously been busy this afternoon. That sounded like hell to me. "Well, how did it feel?"

"It sucked," she admitted. "I felt like I was going to die. Then, when it was over with, I felt exhilarated. I realized I had an enigma."

"An enigma?"

"Yeah, you know, when you realize you know what you want to do with the rest of your life."

"You mean an epiphany," I corrected her.

"Whatever," Lexie muttered. She hated it when I corrected her grammar. I knew it was annoying, but I just couldn't help myself. "I had an epiphany, and this is the way I want to spend the rest of my life."

"Crawling on the floor and doing irreparable bodily harm to yourself?"

"You don't have to make fun of my life ambitions."

She had a point. "Well, I'm glad you had a good day."

"I think you should go with me when you get out of work tomorrow," she said.

Um, no. "Yeah, I don't know if I'll have time," I lied.

"Are you going out with Eliot tomorrow?"

"I don't know how long I'll be at work. We have a big story going on and I'm going to be doing some legwork on it tomorrow."

"Is that true, or do you just not want to do hot yoga?"

It could be true, but I really had no inclination to sweat for no good reason. I'm one of those people that doesn't tolerate heat very well. When it his 80 degrees I have a hard time doing anything but laying on the couch with a fan blowing air directly on me.

"I'll let you know tomorrow," I said. "If I can make it home, I'll go with you." Something told me that some catastrophe would cause me to miss any time period that hot yoga was available.

"I think you should promise me that you'll go," Lexie argued.

"Why?"

"That way there's a fifty percent chance that you'll actually go."

I'm fairly certain she was calling me a liar. "Fine, I promise to try and go."

Lexie stopped what she was doing and shot a glance back at me. "That means you won't go. I know you."

"I said I'll do the best that I can," I shot back. "I'm not going to make a promise when I don't know how my day is going to go."

"Fine," Lexie said shortly.

"Fine."

We both lapsed into silence for a few minutes. "What do you want to do for dinner?" I finally asked.

"We could cook," she suggested. "I got a recipe for vegan pizza while I was at the gym."

"Yeah, I was thinking more like we'd go out for Middle Eastern." Vegan pizza? Pizza without cheese? Yeah, I'm not eating that.

Lexie brightened considerably. "Yeah, Middle Eastern sounds good. Plus, the curry is good for you."

"Plus, it tastes good."

"There is that, too," she conceded.

Vegan pizza my ass.

Sixteen

The next morning, I decided to go to Detroit instead of the office. I wanted to get a feeling for Sarah Frank's work environment. And, if I left directly from my house, I wouldn't have to worry about bringing Duncan with me. It's not just that Duncan is a royal douche. No, really, it isn't. I didn't want to tip my hand that I thought something even bigger was going on here, and that the sheriff's department was hiding information from the public. That would turn into a big deal at the office – and I wasn't ready for that.

I emailed Fish and told him what I was doing. If he remembered that he had ordered me to include Duncan, he didn't mention it. Of course, I didn't bring Duncan up either.

I Googled the location of the office building on my laptop before I left and then programmed the address of the insurance office into my cell phone. I've lived in the Detroit area for years – but I get lost almost every time I go to the city. I'm directionally challenged – at least that's what my dad told me when he was trying to teach me how to drive as a teenager. That's when he wasn't muttering about women being menaces behind the wheel, that is.

Luckily for me, the office building was located in the general vicinity of the Renaissance Center downtown so things were well marked – and relatively safe – for the city of Detroit.

I paid for parking, figuring the $5 would be worth it if I didn't have to walk too far. Parking in Detroit is always an issue. Then I made my way up to the building. I had dressed in flattering black and white Capri pants and a simple black top in anticipation of the office setting I would stepping in to. I didn't figure my standard *Star Wars* clothing would make a good impression for what I was about to do.

When I entered the building, I found that a secretary was sitting behind a desk in the reception area. She looked at me expectantly when I entered. "Can I help you?"

I introduced myself to the secretary and told her I was trying to find someone that knew Sarah Frank. The woman seemed surprised. "We heard that she was missing," she clucked. "I figured she would have shown up by now, though."

"She hasn't," I said. "Her husband is launching an all out media blitz trying to find her."

"She had two kids, right?" The secretary asked. I saw the nameplate on her desk, identifying her as Wanda.

"Yes, Wanda," I smiled warmly. "She had two precious children and we're trying to help find her so she can get back to those children."

That's not a lie. I did hope she would be found. I didn't think it would happen, but I did hope she had simply just decided to take a break from her husband for a couple of weeks and would wander home.

Wanda lowered her voice in a conspiratorial whisper. "No one here is surprised that she took off," she said.

This is why I'm always nice to secretaries. They always have the good dirt. "Really? Most people in her neighborhood don't seem to think she would just take off and leave her kids."

"I don't think she spent much time with those kids," Wanda said. "From what everyone says, her husband was the primary caregiver – and she was the breadwinner."

"Did you think that caused problems in the marriage?" I pretended I was just interested in idle gossip at this point. I couldn't quote the secretary, and that wasn't my ultimate aim. I was just trying to get a candid feel for Sarah Frank when she was in her work environment.

"Yeah, I heard that he called her screaming at her practically every day because he didn't think she paid enough attention to the kids," Wanda said knowingly. "That's why it never works out when the man stays at home."

"What do you mean?"

"It emasculates them. Men can't take it."

I couldn't help but agree with her – at least a little.

"Did he ever come here and make a scene?"

Wanda mulled the question. "I don't remember ever seeing him. In fact, when I saw him on the television the other day I remember thinking that I never pictured him that way."

"What do you mean?"

"His eyes bug out of his head. He's weird looking."

"Yeah, it's even creepier in person," I said.

"There's a rumor going around," Wanda looked around to see if anyone else was listening. "People here think that the husband killed her."

"Why? Because he was sick of taking care of the kids?"

"Well, and the fact that she was sleeping with Dick."

"Who is Dick?"

"The big boss," Wanda supplied. "He's the manager of the entire office."

"Really?" Well, this was news. It didn't actually surprise me, though. I figured those business trips had to be code for something.

"Is Dick the guy she was supposed to go on the trip with?"

"Yes," Wanda said. She was clearly warming to the conversation. "They went on trips together at least once a month."

"Did the trips always last for a week?"

"I don't know about always, but usually."

"How do you know that they're sleeping together?" It could just be office conjecture. The problem with office conjecture, though, is that it is almost always rooted in some form of truth.

"It started about a year ago," Wanda said. "At first, they would just go to lunch together. They made a point of leaving separately and coming back separately, but everyone knew. In fact, Jim in sales said he actually saw them at a restaurant together one day and they looked really chummy."

"When did the trips start?"

"There was always some form of travel for Sarah," Wanda answered. "Dick didn't start going on the trips with her until six months ago. That's when everyone knew for sure that something was going on."

"Did Sarah ever tell anyone that was what was going on?" I believed Wanda, but it was still just office gossip at this point.

"I don't know," Wanda admitted. "Sarah was kind of a loner. When all the women in the office would go out for a ladies night once a month she would never go. She always made up some excuse."

"Was she unfriendly?"

"Not really," Wanda said. "More like she was just standoffish. She wasn't mean or anything," she said hurriedly.

"All her neighbors said she was a great woman," I agreed. "She didn't seem to have a best friend or anything that I've heard of, though. Did you know of anyone?"

"No. Like I said, she did her own thing. The only person she showed any interest in here was Dick. Everyone loves Dick."

I kept my internal chuckle to myself and plowed on. "How has Dick been since she went missing?"

"Really depressed. I think he thinks she's dead."

"Was it unusual for her to just not show up to work for a week?" That was the part of the story that was really niggling me.

"No, that's the thing, she never even called in sick. She was a great employee. She was never even late."

"So why didn't Dick report her missing? Or call the house to check on her?"

"I don't know," Wanda said honestly. "Maybe he didn't want to risk talking to her husband?"

That was a definite possibility.

"You never heard any whispers about Brian Frank threatening her – or that he knew about the affair, did you?"

Wanda shook her head; her blonde curls swinging due to the vigorous motion. "No. We all wondered if he knew. If he did, though, he never came here to confront Dick, so we figured he just didn't know."

"What exactly did Sarah do here? I know you guys do insurance, but why would she be travelling for that?"

"Insurance is a really competitive business," Wanda supplied. "I think they were trying to get international customers."

"Is that unusual?"

"Not in this business market. I think most insurance companies do it."

Well, that was a dead end. "But do they do it in the Bahamas?"

"There are a lot of rich people that live in the Bahamas," Wanda pointed out. "If they landed a really big client then it could fund the entire business for a whole year."

"Did they land any big clients?"

"They did, two in the last year at least. We held parties when it happened."

"So she was good at her job?"

"She was really good at her job, I think," Wanda said. "No one ever said anything bad about her."

"Well, that's good." Despite the tidbit about the affair with the boss, I really hadn't learned anything. "Did she get bonuses when she signed a new client?"

"Yeah, whoever signs a client gets some form of bonus. It's usually contingent on how big the account is."

Well, that made sense.

"That's how she could afford to hire an au pair," Wanda added.

Wait, what? My eyebrows nearly shot off my head. This was the first I was hearing about this. "An au pair? What au pair?"

"It's a babysitter," Wanda said simply.

"I know what an au pair is. I didn't know she had one, though. I've never seen her. Where is she from?"

"I thinks he's a young woman from Germany," Wanda said. "I remember hearing Sarah say that she thought the kids liked Steffi more than her."

"The au pair's name is Steffi?"

"Yeah."

"And you're sure she was still working for them?"

"I'm pretty sure. Just two weeks ago I heard Sarah telling one of the other women that getting the au pair was one of the best things she ever did because it was helping Brian to relax a little bit and freeing him up to do some sort of projects at home."

"What kind of projects?" I had no idea what Brian Frank did for a living – if he did anything. He had mentioned working from home, but I figured that was his code for being a house husband.

"I have no idea. Whatever they were, Sarah always made fun of them," Wanda said. "She said they were a waste of time but they made him feel better so she encouraged him to do them."

Huh.

"And how long have they had the au pair?"

"At least two months."

Secretaries really are invaluable in situations like this. I thanked Wanda for her time and moved to leave the building. I stopped and turned back when a thought occurred to me. "Is Dick in the office?"

"No, he's on another trip."

"Alone?"

"To my knowledge."

Things just got a whole heck of a lot more interesting.

Seventeen

After I left the office, I sat in my car outside the building and watched the people that entered and left for about an hour. They didn't seem any different than any other people – not that I expected them to suddenly morph into werewolves or something. What I was really looking for was Dick. No, not that way. Before I had left the reception area I caught sight of a picture on the wall, identifying Richard C. Norton, office manager. He wasn't exactly what I expected, but his eyes didn't bug out of his head at an odd angle, either. He was about fifty years old, with salt-and-pepper dark hair and a nice smile. He wasn't exactly handsome, but he wasn't ugly either. Since he was in a powerful position, I figured that would make him that much more attractive to Sarah.

It wasn't that I didn't believe Wanda, but I just wanted to make sure Dick was really out of town. Once lunch time had passed, and I still hadn't seen Dick (pun intended), I gave up and headed back home to Roseville.

I was going to spend the afternoon at home before attending a candlelight vigil out at the Frank house this evening. When I checked my email at my house, Fish had informed me that Duncan would be driving himself out to Romeo himself and covering the candlelight vigil with his point-of-view camera. Great.

I was happily watching *General Hospital* when I heard the back door open. Lexie had been gone for her shift at Starbucks when I got up, so I wasn't surprised that she was getting home so early in the afternoon.

"You're home," she said.

"I noticed," I shot back dryly.

"I thought you were going to be busy all afternoon?"

"I did what I had to do this morning, and now I'm done until the candlelight vigil tonight," I replied.

"When is that?"

"It starts at 8 p.m. Why?"

"Because now you have no excuse not to go to yoga with me," Lexie said happily.

Shit.

I opened my mouth to start arguing, but one look at Lexie's face told me that would be a fruitless endeavor. I reluctantly got to my feet and disappeared into my bedroom. When I came back out fifteen minutes later, I found Lexie had already changed into stretch pants and a tank top.

She looked me up and down for a second and then shook her head. "I can't believe you actually found *Star Wars* yoga pants."

"It wasn't easy," I lamented. "This is the first time I've worn them, though."

"I can see why."

Whatever.

Lexie and I decided to walk to the gym since it was only two blocks away. Since it was early autumn, the days were still warm and the walk was actually nice. "Can't we just count this as our workout?"

"No."

When I entered the gym, I was even more horrified than I initially thought I would be. The room was painted a violent shade of pink, and there were bead curtains draped across store shelves that hocked everything from green tea to incense. I knew it was a front for a drug den.

Lexie didn't seem to notice the incredulous look on my face. She greeted two women behind the counter amiably. "Destiny, Dove, this is my cousin Avery. I told her how great the class was and talked her into coming."

Destiny and Dove? Great.

I nodded at them in greeting, but I didn't want to get too close. I wasn't sure, but I was fairly certain that pompous preening wasn't contagious. I didn't want to take any chances, though.

If you ever have the chance to do hot yoga – don't. That's the best piece of advice I can give you – ever. When I equated it with hell, I wasn't far off. Picture sitting in a room that is as hot as a furnace and having some tiny little drill sergeant barking at you to position your arms and legs into positions that are virtually impossible. Yeah, it's that bad.

After about twenty minutes of it, I was done. I got to my feet and turned to leave the building.

"Where are you going?" Lexie hissed.

"I'm not staying here. This is even worse than I thought it would be."

"You're embarrassing me."

"I'd rather embarrass you than sweat to death," I replied.

I didn't bother looking back. By the time I got to the street, I started to see stars. I sat down at the curb until my head started to feel like the spinning was controllable and then walked the rest of the way home.

I took a cold shower and then slept for an hour. When I woke up, I took another shower and got ready for the candlelight vigil.

I texted Eliot to ask if he was going to be at the candlelight vigil. He responded that he was, and then asked me if I wanted to spend the night at his place. It sounded pretty tempting, so I said yes.

I left a note for Lexie telling her I wasn't coming home tonight, packed a small bag with clothes for work tomorrow and then headed out to the candlelight vigil. When I got out to the Frank house, I wasn't surprised to see that the whole media circus had descended on Romeo. This was officially the biggest story in the area. Pretty soon the locusts and vermin would arrive – and then Nancy Grace.

I parked my car down the street and made my way through the hundreds of people who had gathered in front of the house. I couldn't imagine that all of these people actually knew Sarah – but the American public is a glutton for an overt spectacle.

I saw Duncan standing by a tree. He had some weird band on his head with one of the most laughably ugly cameras strapped to it. What a tool. I purposely avoided him and instead took in the assembled crowd for a few minutes.

I could see a small contingent of sheriff's deputies milling about with the crowd in uniform. I noticed that Jake was one of them.

He was standing in the center of everyone and greeting people as they approached him. This is Macomb County, so other than a few white rappers, Jake is the closest thing we have to a celebrity. It's a little ridiculous.

As I glanced down the street, I could see that trucks from all four of the networks were on hand. I recognized representatives from several dailies in the area – some out of the county – and several weekly reporters, as well.

"This is unbelievable," I heard a voice whisper in my ear.

I smiled at Eliot in greeting. "Is this your first media circus?"

"The first one I've seen up close."

Eliot dropped a kiss on the corner of my mouth and continued to scan the crowd. "What are you looking for?"

"Just looking," he said simply.

I didn't believe him, but I figured it wasn't exactly any of my business. "What did you do today?" He asked.

"I went down and talked to some people at Sarah Frank's office – and then I went to hell with Lexie."

"Did the office workers tell you anything?"

"Some stuff," I hedged. I wasn't sure how much I wanted to tell him.

"You're not going to tell me?" He was smiling at me.

"I haven't decided yet," I said honestly.

"Well, then I guess I won't tell you what I know either," Eliot teased.

"Why? What do you know?"

"What will you give me to find out?" Eliot grabbed my hand and pulled me closer to him.

"What do you want? I already said I was going home with you?"

"This is true. I didn't even have to twist your arm."

"How about we agree to share information later tonight and not here in front of everyone?"

"That sounds like a good idea," Eliot agreed, letting me move away from his chest. "I don't think either one of us wants to talk in front of all these vultures."

I let the vulture comment slide. In most respects, he was right. There were very few reporters I could stand – myself included -- and none of them were here.

"Look at that idiot with the camera strapped on his head." Eliot was pointing to Duncan, but my attention was fixated on Jake, who was greeting a woman with a Channel 7 microphone. From behind, I could have swore it was Shelly. When she turned so I could see her profile, I realized that it definitely was Shelly. I swore under my breath.

"What?" Eliot followed the direction of my gaze. He frowned when he saw what I was looking at.

"It's Jake, so what?"

"Not Jake, the woman he's with."

"The new Channel 7 reporter, Shelly Waters?"

"You know who she is?"

"She's hot." Eliot must have realized what he said, because he turned a sheepish grin in my direction. "Not as hot as you, though."

Right.

"What's your problem with her?"

"I have a problem with all television reporters," I reminded him.

"Right. They take credit for the work while actual reporters do the work," he mimicked me in a high pitched voice.

"That's not how I sound," I snapped.

Eliot glanced at me out of the corner of his eye. He could tell I was agitated. "So, what's your problem with her?"

Whoops. How was I going to explain that? Screw it, might as well tell the truth. "She's Jake's girlfriend."

"Really?" Eliot raised his eyebrows. "How do you know that? Did Jake tell you that at lunch yesterday?" It was the first time he'd brought up lunch. I decided to ignore the question.

"Lexie and I saw them at breakfast on Sunday," I said.

"So?"

"So? So he's going to give her favorable treatment," I complained.

"Like the favorable treatment he's given you for years?" Eliot's gaze was steady. Jake had been a sore spot between us since we met. I couldn't help but wonder if he was rethinking his choice to date me.

"Oh, please, I didn't get favorable treatment. I got threats and ominous warnings."

"I think maybe you see it differently than everybody else."

He could be right.

I saw another television reporter join Jake and Shelly. It was Devon, Derrick's dingbat girlfriend. Could my day get any worse? I shouldn't have asked that, because the other television reporter, Ariel, joined the small group. I could hear them all laughing jovially with each other.

"Oh, great," I moaned. "It's the confederacy of dunces."

Eliot's eyes sparkled as he watched my anger. "I think that you have a weird thing about television reporters, and maybe it's not healthy."

"They're assholes," I complained.

"No, that guy over there with the camera strapped to his head is an asshole."

I glanced over at Duncan and grimaced as I saw him trying to interview people with the camera. That was going to be some gripping footage – if you were blind and deaf.

Jake had caught sight of Eliot and me. He did a half wave. Shelly turned to see who he was looking at, and when she caught sight of me I saw her face darken. I guess my reputation still proceeded me in media circles.

Jake made his way over to us, greeting us formally. "Ms. Shaw. Mr. Kane."

Sheriff Dumbass. "Jake."

"This turned into a big deal, huh?"

"Yeah," Eliot looked around at the crowd again. "I'm surprised so many people came out."

"People feel the need to be part of the news when they can," I pointed out.

"You're awful cynical," Shelly had joined Jake, putting a possessive hand on his arm.

"I am," I agreed.

"You should have more faith in humanity."

"What are you? A fortune cookie?"

Jake bit the inside of his lip. I could feel Eliot shifting uncomfortably next to me. Shelly decided to ignore my jab. "And who is this handsome gentleman?"

Eliot extended his hand and introduced himself. "So you're the private investigator working for Mr. Frank?" Shelly looked interested. I could tell Jake was uncomfortable with the interest.

"I am," Eliot answered easily.

"Would you be willing to do an exclusive interview with me on what you've turned up?"

"No."

Jake and I both looked at Eliot in surprise. I wasn't surprised that he declined, but the fact that he was so succinct while doing it did take me off guard.

"Why?" Shelly wasn't going to be deterred.

"I'm not here to be a media correspondent," Eliot answered shortly.

"You're talking to Ms. Shaw?" She pointed out.

"He's sleeping with Ms. Shaw," Jake grumbled. "There's a difference."

Shelly looked surprised, while I shot Jake a dirty look. "You're sleeping with *her*?"

What was that supposed to mean?

"I guess I am," Eliot responded dryly. "I'm not doing interviews with her either, though."

Shelly looked suddenly smug. "Does she know that?"

"She didn't even ask, so I would guess so." Eliot was looking decidedly uncomfortable.

This conversation was just too surreal for me at this point. "I better go talk to some people in the crowd."

"Yeah, me too," Shelly said warily.

I turned back to Eliot. "I'll see you after the vigil and just follow you back to town."

Eliot nodded, but he was eying Shelly with open distaste. If I had to guess, he'd be jumping on my television reporter hate brigade before the night was out.

I saw Jake frown as he regarded the two of us, and then he turned on his heel and stalked away.

Fun times in Romeo.

Eighteen

After the candlelight vigil – which felt like it went on for hours – I waited for Eliot out on the front lawn while he went inside the Frank house for a few minutes. He didn't tell me what he was doing, and I had the good sense not to ask.

As I paced, I saw Duncan start to approach me. Great.

"I got some great footage," he said excitedly.

"Good for you."

Duncan furrowed his brow as he regarded me. I couldn't help but notice – with a grim sense of satisfaction – that he was getting some gray hairs in his eyebrows. Since Duncan was terrified of growing old, I figured he hadn't noticed them yet. "Aren't you going to write your story?"

"I already did. I wrote it on my iPad in the car and sent it off."

Duncan looked surprised. "Don't you think you should look at my video and tailor your story to fit my video."

I can't think of anything I'd rather not do. "No."

"Well, I'm going to talk to Fish about this."

"You do that."

"Why are you still here if you're done?" Duncan asked suspiciously.

"I'm waiting for someone."

"Who?"

"None of your business."

"If you're hiding stuff from me, Fish isn't going to be happy."

"Fish is never happy."

I was looking everywhere but at Duncan. Couldn't he take a hint? I so did not want to be seen with him and his stupid little camera — which was still on his forehead, by the way.

"I think you're hiding something," Duncan shot back.

"No, I'm pretty sure I've made my disdain for you pretty overt."

I saw that Jake was watching Duncan and me curiously. He started moving towards us, and Duncan started preening like a pigeon when he saw it. "Jake Farrell is coming over here."

"I'll alert the media."

Duncan ignored me and took a step towards Jake excitedly. "Sheriff Farrell, I'm Duncan Marlow."

Jake regarded him with mild amusement. "I know who you are."

"You do?"

"Avery has told me . . . some things."

Duncan shot an angry glance at me. "I'm sure they were slanderous."

"After seeing the camera and talking to you for less than a minute, I'm thinking she was probably telling the truth," Jake shot back.

Duncan makes friends wherever he goes. And, despite my general anger with Jake these days, I couldn't help but love him a little bit for bitch slapping Duncan in a public setting. I didn't think Duncan would be able to haul Jake down to human resources.

Duncan's brown eyes darkened harshly. "I think you should know, Avery is a pathological liar and anything she's told you is both slanderous and . . . "

"I really don't care," Jake interrupted. "Now, if you don't mind, I need to talk to Avery alone for a minute."

Duncan's mouth dropped open. "I'm working on this story with her."

"I don't want to talk to her about the story," Jake shot back.

"Then what do you want to talk to her about?"

"How is that any of your business?"

"Duncan thinks everything is his business," I answered.

"Well, this isn't," Jake replied, brushing his hand in a wave motion to get Duncan to walk away.

Duncan did slink away, but the glance he shot back at me was chilling. He was going to try and make me pay for this, I was sure.

When he was gone, Jake turned back to me. "That guy is a douche."

"I know." Everyone knows.

"Are you waiting for Eliot?"

"Yeah," I said. There really was no reason to lie when he already knew the truth.

"Where is he?"

"In the house."

"Other than the candlelight vigil, what did you do today?"

That was a pointed question. "Just some legwork on the story. Then Lexie and I went to hot yoga this afternoon.'

Jake smiled despite himself. "I can't imagine you at hot yoga."

"It wasn't pretty," I admitted.

"I bet."

Jake looked out at the now empty lawn. The only people still hanging around were the media. I noticed that Shelly was standing over by her news van. She was watching Jake and me talk – and she didn't look happy.

"What legwork did you do?"

Jake was digging for information. He wanted to know what I uncovered. I had no intention of telling him. "Just a few people I wanted to talk to," I said evasively.

"Like who?"

"Just some people."

"You're not going to tell me?"

"Nope."

Jake and I both looked up when we heard a door shut. Eliot was walking across the lawn in my direction. He made his way towards us. "Are you ready to go?" He asked me.

"Yeah."

Jake regarded Eliot a second. "What's your take on this guy?"

I was surprised by the question. Eliot wasn't, though. "I don't know," he said truthfully. "He seems like he's telling the truth, but the whole thing is off."

"Do you think she's dead?"

"Probably," Eliot said. "We can't really be sure, though, can we?"

"No," Jake agreed. He turned and cast a wary glance in my direction. "Watch her," he said finally. "If this guy is a murderer – or even if he isn't – she's bound to get in some sort of trouble if she's not watched."

"I know," Eliot said. "I'll do what I can."

"I'm standing right here, you know?" Unbelievable.

"I know," Jake said before turning and walking away.

I followed Eliot to his place, parking in front of the pawnshop and heading up to Eliot's apartment above the store. I had spent the night here before, but it hadn't been in the same capacity. This would be the first time we stayed at his place together, and I was suddenly nervous.

Eliot was already upstairs when I arrived. He took my overnight bag from me and put it in his bedroom. Then he went into the kitchen, poured us each a glance of wine and then joined me on the couch in the living room. "I want to talk to you – and I don't want you to freak out."

"That's a great conversation starter," I joked.

"This is still kind of new, but I know you well enough to feel that if I tell you not to investigate this story that's only going to make you more determined to investigate this story."

That was definitely true.

"So," he continued. "I need you to be careful."

"You think he killed her, don't you?"

"I think he's a weird guy," Eliot said cautiously.

"Is that because his eyes bug out of his head like he's trying to take a dump or because his wife was having an affair?" I decided to go for broke.

Eliot didn't look surprised. I figured he already knew. "Is that what you were doing today? Investigating the affair?"

"Actually, I was just fishing. The affair information just kind of fell in my lap."

"Who told you?"

"A secretary at her office."

"You sweet talked a secretary for gossip?" Eliot looked impressed.

"I'm good at my job."

"I don't doubt it. What else did this secretary tell you?"

"Just that Sarah Frank was a loner who only spent time with the boss, Dick."

"Yeah, he's been out of the country all week," Eliot said. "I've been trying to track him down."

"Where is he?"

"The Bahamas," Eliot said. "I don't know exactly where, though."

"Are you going to go there and talk to him?"

"No," Eliot said. "I don't want to be that far away if you get in trouble."

That was sweet – and condescending. "I've been taking care of myself for a really long time," I reminded him.

"In the few months I've known you, you've been taken hostage by a madman and held at gunpoint by a deranged stripper. I'm not taking any chances."

I decided to ignore the statement – even if it did make me feel a rush of affection for him. "Have you met the au pair?"

Eliot looked surprised. "How do you know about the au pair?"

That rush of affection fled as fast as it came. "Why didn't you tell me about the au pair?"

"I didn't think it mattered."

"A young woman living in the house who might have seen something? You don't think that matters?"

"I don't think she knows anything," Eliot said simply.

"Have the police talked to her?"

"Yes."

So Jake was a liar, too. "Do the police know about the affair?"

"Yes."

"I knew it! I knew he was lying to me."

"Isn't that his job?"

Whatever. "Do you think he killed her?"

"I think she's dead," Eliot said. "Of course, she could also be in the Bahamas with her boss."

I had wondered that briefly myself.

"Most of the people I've talked to don't seem to think she would just abandon the kids," I said.

"Unless there's something else about their marriage that we don't know about."

He had a point.

Eliot slid a sly glance in my direction. "Any more questions?"

"Not right now."

"Good. Let's go to bed. I've got things I'd rather be discussing in there with you."

I couldn't help it, I felt a little thrill. We'd done enough work for tonight.

Nineteen

When I got to the office the next morning, I was feeling relaxed and satiated – despite the stressful situation from the night before. What can I say? Eliot is good at taking my mind off things.

When I got to the office, Fish called me over to his desk. He slid a piece of paper towards me. It looked like a press release from the sheriff's department. I was surprised when I read it.

"You've got to be kidding," I muttered. "They're holding daily press conferences now?"

"Yeah," Fish replied. "I thought it was odd, too."

"At least they're holding the press conferences at the sheriff's department instead of out at the house." That meant a five minute drive instead of a half-hour one.

"This whole thing is just weird," Fish finally said. "What have you found out?"

"What do you mean?"

"Don't be cute. I know you have been tracking stuff down. What have you got?"

I told Fish about the affair and the au pair, making sure to keep my voice low. I didn't want everyone in the room to hear me. We're a gossipy bunch. Fish didn't seem surprised. He had been in the news business for forty years. We'd heard it all at this point. "What is your next move?"

I shrugged. "I'll go to the press conference and then decide from there."

"I'm sending Duncan to the press conference to video it."

Great. "I'm not taking him with me to do interviews," I warned Fish. "No one is going to tell me anything with that asshole by my side."

"I know. We'll keep him busy with the video. I'll send him out to the house to get B-footage this afternoon to keep him busy."

I wanted to ask Fish what the sudden push to have Duncan do video was, but I didn't want to piss him off since he was finally talking to me again. "That's a good idea," I said finally.

Fish smiled at me for the first time in a month. "As long as you don't have to deal with him, you don't care."

That was true.

I sat down at my desk long enough to check my emails, but there wasn't anything interesting in my inbox. I grabbed a fresh notebook and headed off to the sheriff's department. I wanted to get there early enough to talk to Derrick – without the other media muddying the water.

The sheriff's department is only a few minutes away from the newspaper office, so I stopped at an area coffee shop to get a shot of caffeine before I headed over. When I got to the sheriff's department, I stopped at the protective bubble to announce my presence. Like most law enforcement offices these days, you can't just wander around the sheriff's department. You have to be buzzed in to the inner sanctum.

"You're early," the petulant female officer on the other side of the glass informed me. "The press conference doesn't start for another half an hour."

"I know. I just love law enforcement and I can't spend enough time around you guys," I shot back sarcastically.

The officer gave me a dour look, but she buzzed me in anyway. I was familiar with the halls of the sheriff's department, so I made my way down to Derrick's office – which was open – and looked inside. He was sitting at his desk. "Hey," I greeted him.

"You're early," he didn't bother looking up.

"So I've been told."

"What do you want?"

"Can't I just want to visit my favorite cousin?"

"Lexie is your favorite cousin."

"Well, you're her brother, so you're favorite cousin adjacent."

"How is she, by the way? I heard she's staying with you until she finds a place."

"She's already got a job at Starbucks – and she's got a new passion in life."

"I'm afraid to ask," Derrick grimaced. "What is her new passion?"

"She wants to be a yoga instructor."

Derrick considered that for a second. "She might be good at that," he said finally. "It's a lot better than some of her other passions."

"You mean like when she moved to Florida for two years and thought she was Cuban and wanted to organize rescue boats to save Cuban refugees from the ocean?"

"Yeah, like that."

"She made me go to hot yoga yesterday," I said.

"That must have gone over well. You hate being hot."

"I lasted twenty minutes and then bailed," I admitted.

"I wouldn't have lasted that long. That sounds like hell."

"You have no idea."

I slid into the chair across from Derrick's desk. He watched me with a bemused expression.

"So, what's going on with the Frank case?"

"You'll find out at the press conference," he said briefly, turning back to his paperwork.

"Come on, give your cousin a little tidbit," I pleaded.

"No."

"Do all of your co-workers know that you wore a dress for Halloween?" When all else fails, blackmail is always a viable option.

Derrick narrowed his eyes as he regarded me. "I doubt my co-workers care what I did when I was a small child."

"You were in college," I corrected him.

"That was a fraternity dare," he shot back.

"Not when I get done telling it, it won't be."

"You wouldn't tell people that," a voice from the hallway said.

Derrick and I both turned to see Jake standing in the doorway regarding us. "You don't know that," I scoffed.

"Please. You guys bag on each other constantly, but you wouldn't really turn on him. You're too loyal. You both are."

"I think you're giving her too much credit," Derrick said. "She told Devon that she wasn't sure I was straight until I started bringing her to family dinner."

Jake raised his eyebrows. "You did that?"

What? I don't like her. "I didn't say anything that wasn't true."

"Right."

I turned to Jake irritably. "Shouldn't you be doing your hair so you're camera ready?"

"I'm always camera ready," he replied calmly. "I'm naturally pretty."

"I wouldn't go around announcing that," I told him.

"I'm comfortable with my masculinity."

"Of course you are," a saccharine voice emanated from the hallway behind Jake. He turned and smiled when he saw Shelly standing behind him.

"Hey," Jake greeted her warmly. "You look really nice."

"Thank you."

I rolled my eyes and looked over at Derrick. He was watching me for my reaction. I stuck my tongue out at him in response.

"What is everyone doing?" Shelly asked. Her tone never shifted, but I could tell she was a little uncomfortable finding Jake with me – again.

"Talking about the merits of men wearing dresses," I said smoothly.

"Like kilts?" Shelly looked confused.

"No, like chiffon."

Derrick shot me a dark look, while Jake shook his head in my direction. "The press conference will be starting in a few minutes. Why don't we all go over to the conference room?"

Shelly smiled at Jake obligingly. "Of course."

"I'll be there in a second," I said. "I need to talk to Derrick about something."

"What?" Shelly asked suspiciously.

"Family stuff."

"Meaning?" Shelly obviously didn't like me. I didn't blame her. The feeling was entirely mutual.

"Meaning you're not family," I shot back.

Jake grabbed Shelly by the elbow and started to lead her away. "Behave," he admonished me.

Once he was gone, I turned back to Derrick. I was running out of time. "I heard you guys talked to the au pair?"

"How do you know about the au pair?"

"I'm omnipotent."

"I didn't believe that when we were eight and you kept telling people you were really a magical alien, and I don't believe it now."

"A little birdie told me," I tried again.

"She doesn't know anything," Derrick said finally. "She's a dead end. Don't waste your time."

He's hiding something.

"Okay," I said, getting to my feet. "I believe you."

"That's your lying voice," Derrick replied.

"It's no different than your lying voice," I countered.

Derrick and I eyed each other carefully. We were at an impasse. Unfortunately, this wasn't an unusual scenario for us.

I left Derrick's office and went into the conference room. Most of the television reporters and newspaper representatives were already present. I helped myself to a donut and then made my way over to Tony Winters. "How's it going?"

"Good," Tony said. "I can't believe how big this story is blowing up."

"Me either," I said. "It must be a slow news cycle."

"It's getting national mentions now," Tony said. "Nancy Grace mentioned it on her show last night."

I knew it.

"She's asked me to be on her show tonight," I heard a voice behind me say. I turned to see Shelly standing behind me with a smug look on her face.

"Good for you."

"This is a big deal," Shelly said. "Jake and I are going to be on a national news program together. That's a big step for us."

"Will you be naked?"

"What?" Shelly furrowed her brow.

"Just curious."

Tony was smiling at our exchange. Everyone likes a girl fight.

"What is your deal?" Shelly asked me angrily.

"What do you mean?"

"You have an attitude with me."

"Avery has an attitude with everyone," Tony supplied.

Shelly shot him a dirty look. Tony looked appropriately abashed and walked away. I could see him heading directly for Derrick in the corner. Probably warning him that I was about to throw down.

"I want to know what your problem is," Shelly repeated.

"I don't have a problem. I just don't like you."

"You don't even know me."

"I don't like all television reporters. Don't take it personally," I said flippantly.

"I think it's more than that. I think you're jealous because I'm with Jake."

"You're entitled to your opinion."

"You're not denying it."

"I don't deny being an elf either. That doesn't mean it's true."

Shelly looked confused again. "What does that have to do with anything?"

Derrick was making his way across the room towards us. He was clearly worried. He should be.

"Listen, Shelly, you're not my problem. Let's just agree to stay away from each other."

"That's not a problem for me, but you seem incapable of staying away from my boyfriend."

"That sounds like a problem for you and Jake to discuss," Derrick interjected, moving to my side.

"I'm discussing it with her."

"This isn't the place to discuss it," Derrick replied. He was clearly angry. "Maybe you should pick a playground and fight it out there."

Shelly shot Derrick a disgusted look. "Your whole family is nuts, from what I've read. It shouldn't surprise me that you're taking her side."

"She doesn't need me to take her side," Derrick replied curtly. "She's more than capable of doing it on her own. " Derrick took a step towards Shelly. "And you're not equipped to take her on. She'll eat you for lunch and still have room for dessert."

Shelly narrowed her eyes and regarded him. "I'm telling Jake that you're disrespecting me in favor of your low-class cousin."

Oh, I was in this now. "Why don't you do that," I seethed. "Why don't you go tell him that I was being mean to you and see what that gets you?"

Shelly shifted her gaze between Derrick and me for a second. She seemed to be collecting herself. "This isn't over," she said finally before turning on her heel and stalking away.

"I can't wait for the encore."

Twenty

After the press conference – which equated to a big pile of nothing – I was getting ready to leave the sheriff's department when Derrick approached me. "Come to my office," he said in a low whisper.

I followed Derrick dutifully. I was still reeling from him coming to my aid in the Shelly fight. When we got to his office, Derrick closed the door behind us. "Are you alright?"

"I'm fine. I didn't need you to ride in with your white hat – even though I appreciate it."

"I don't like her," Derrick said finally. That was pretty much as close to a compliment – and cease fire -- as we were going to be able to maintain.

"What did you want to tell me?" I asked him, changing the subject.

"I can't give you specifics," Derrick said. "You know that."

"Then why did you call me in here?"

"I wanted to make sure that she was gone before you left," he said honestly. "I didn't want to have another crime scene in the parking lot if I could help it. You'd beat the shit out of her and then I'd get stuck with the paperwork – and explaining to your mom why you're spending the night in jail."

Yeah, no one wanted that.

"By the way, can you get her to stop texting me?"

"No, I can't get her to stop texting me," I said ruefully.

"She's starting to follow me around on Facebook, too," Derrick added.

"Get used to that."

Derrick sighed. He knew there was nothing I could do, so I don't know why he would even ask.

"Are you guys watching Brian Frank?" I changed topics.

"We're investigating the case," Derrick said evasively.

"That means yes."

"That means we're investigating the case," Derrick affirmed.

"Are you watching the au pair, too?"

Derrick sighed. "She's probably gone now. It's probably safe for you to leave."

I took the hint and left. I didn't need him to confirm it for me anyway. I knew that the police were holding their cards incredibly close to their vests for a reason. I could figure out why on my own.

I headed back to the office, but not before I looked to see if Shelly was in the parking lot. The Channel 7 news truck was still there – but there was no Shelly in sight. She was probably still inside tattling to Jake. I could only hope Derrick didn't get in any trouble for taking my side. If he did, there was going to be a rather loud fight in the sheriff's personal office in the next few days.

When I got back into the office, I saw that a couple of reporters were grouped around Duncan's desk and watching something on his computer. It was probably that hilarious video about the news reporter going ghetto in the middle of a story on YouTube. We rediscovered it periodically – and it was always funny.

"Nothing new at the press conference," I announced to Fish as I approached his desk.

"So nothing happened at the press conference?" He raised an eyebrow as he regarded me.

Crap. What had Duncan told him?

"No," I said evasively. "Nothing we didn't already know. She's still missing."

"So you didn't get in a fight with the Channel 7 reporter?"

"Define fight."

Fish fixed me with a tired look.

"There might have been some words exchanged," I admitted.

"Why?"

"I don't like her."

"You don't like any television reporters, none of us do, but you usually don't get in big bitch fights with them at the sheriff's department."

Not that he knew of, at least. It's not like it was the first time. Devon and I had exchanged words a few times. Ironically, that had also happened at the sheriff's department. And a couple of crime scenes. And the family restaurant.

"She started it," I protested.

"You didn't have to engage," Fish argued. We both exchanged a look. That wasn't true. I can't stop myself from engaging.

"I'm sorry," I said finally.

"It won't happen again?"

We both knew I couldn't promise that. "It won't happen again . . . I hope."

"Fine," Fish said. "Where do you go from here?"

"I'm going to try and find the au pair," I said simply.

"Do you think it will be that easy?"

"Probably not. I think she knows something, though. That's why the cops are trying to hide her so desperately."

"Is she still working at the house?"

"As far as I know."

I heard the reporters grouped around Duncan's desk laughing maniacally. "What are they looking at? Did Duncan take the point-of-view camera to a Civil War reenactment and forget that the war has been over for more than two hundred years?"

"No," Fish replied. "He taped you fighting with the Channel 7 reporter."

"He did not!"

"He did, and he's showing everyone in the room."

"Why didn't you stop him?"

"Why would I? It's funny."

I hate these people. If that shows up on YouTube, Duncan is going to be sorry.

Twenty-One

After filing my story from today's press conference, I found myself at a loss. Not only was I plotting retribution for Duncan, but I was also at a wall I couldn't quite see over. I needed to learn more about the au pair, but all I had was a first name. I figured I would probably need some help on this. I couldn't go to the police – because they had no intention of helping me – so that left Eliot.

We had agreed to have dinner and spend the night together at his place again. What can I say? He's addictive. Plus, Lexie and her yoga obsession were making my two-bedroom house seem even smaller than it was.

I left work and returned home long enough to pack more clothes in a bag and change my outfit. Eliot hadn't said where we were going, so I settled on simple black pants and a billowy top from Express. I ran my straightening iron over my hair, touched up my makeup, and left a note for Lexie. I didn't know if she was at work or at the gym – but I figured she would be just as relieved to have me out of the house, as I was to be out of it.

I drove to Eliot's place and knocked on the door. He opened it, greeting me with a warm hug and a kiss.

"How was your day?" He asked, taking my bag from me.

"Interesting," I said briefly.

Eliot raised his eyebrows, but he didn't question me further. At least for now. Instead, he led me into the bathroom and opened one of the drawers. It was empty. "I figured you could keep some of your stuff here so you didn't have to keep packing a bag everyday."

"You're giving me a drawer?" I was surprised, and touched.

"It's not a big deal," I could see his cheeks redden slightly. "I emptied out some drawers in the bedroom, too."

"Thanks." I wasn't quite sure what to say to him. It felt like things were moving incredibly fast – and yet it felt comfortable.

Eliot reached into his pocket and pulled out a key. He handed it to me wordlessly.

"What's this?"

"It's a key to the apartment," he said. "I figured that way you could just let yourself in if you need to."

I was stunned. "You trust me in your place? Alone?"

"Why wouldn't I?"

"I'm nosy," I admitted.

"I have nothing to hide."

Eliot and I decided to drive over to Hall Road so we could have a nice seafood dinner. Once we were seated and had ordered, Eliot turned his attention back to me. "So what did you do today?"

"There was a press conference at the sheriff's department."

"Anything new?"

"Absolutely nothing. They're holding daily press conferences there, though."

Eliot looked surprised. "Why?"

"I don't know. The way they're approaching this case is just really odd."

"I agree. They know a lot more than they're saying."

"Derrick says they're keeping surveillance on Brian Frank."

"He told you that?" Eliot looked startled.

"No, he said they're investigating the case, but I could tell by the way he wouldn't answer me."

"Only you would say something like that," Eliot laughed.

"I know him," I said simply. "He can't lie to me. He can evade, but I know when he's lying."

"Does he know when you're lying?" Eliot asked curiously.

"Yep."

"Did anything else happen?" Eliot was eying me purposefully.

Crap. What had he heard? "That's all that happened regarding the case," I said finally.

"So, you didn't get in a fight with Shelly?"

"Who told you that?"

"It's on YouTube."

"I'm going to kill Duncan," I muttered.

"Why were you fighting with her?"

"She started it."

"That's not what I asked."

"She has an issue with me."

"You have an issue with her, too," Eliot pointed out.

"I have an issue with . . . "

"All television reporters, I know," Eliot interrupted. "You really don't like her, though. Is it because of Jake?"

"No," I said. Although, I wasn't sure if that was true. "I don't like the way she's always following me around. Trying to find out what I know. That's not how this business works. We don't do the legwork for each other. We try to win."

"And this is just about winning?"

"Yes."

Eliot let it go. We ate our meal in compatible silence. When we were done, Eliot led me out of the restaurant by my hand. "I want to meet the au pair," I said finally.

"Why?"

"Because I think she knows something."

"What is it with you and the au pair?" Eliot seemed genuinely curious.

"I think it's weird that everyone is trying to keep her a secret. That automatically piques my curiosity."

"I don't think she knows anything," Eliot said.

"Have you questioned her?"

"I've talked to her. She seems like a young girl from another country who is confused by what is going on."

"Is she hot?"

Eliot barked out a laugh. "What does that have to do with anything?"

"It's just a question."

"She's attractive," Eliot ceded. "I don't know if I would call her hot, but she's cute."

"Do you think Brian Frank had anything going on with her?"

Eliot looked surprised. "Why would you ask that?" That wasn't an answer to my question.

"An older man seducing the naïve nanny is an old story," I supplied.

"I haven't seen anything that would make me think they're sleeping together," Eliot said.

"But you have your suspicions?"

Eliot sighed as he looked at me. "You really are better at this than people give you credit for."

"So, they are sleeping together?"

"I don't know that," Eliot cautioned. "I just get a weird vibe from them."

"Like they're humping like bunnies?"

Eliot shook his head, but he couldn't hide his smile. "Maybe," he conceded.

"Have you asked her?"

"You don't just come out and ask something like that," Eliot admonished me.

I would. "Can you arrange a meeting between us?"

"I can try," Eliot said.

That was a start.

Twenty-Two

I woke up in a tangle of arms, legs and a pile of tousled hair. I could feel Eliot breathing deeply beside me. He was still asleep. I took a few minutes to just enjoy the feeling.

"What are you thinking about?"

Apparently Eliot wasn't asleep. "How warm you feel," I said honestly.

"I would have preferred you calling me hot," Eliot teased.

"I don't want your head to get any bigger than it already is."

Eliot and I showered together – which took longer than it probably should – and then we had a quick breakfast of toast and juice standing up at the kitchen counter.

"What are you doing today?" I asked him.

"I'm going out to the Frank house to check in and see if I can get the au pair to talk to you. I'll call you on your cell if I work something out."

"Thanks."

"What are you going to do?"

"I have my now daily briefing at the sheriff's department. After that, I'm not sure."

Eliot walked me downstairs, giving me a quick kiss on the street in front of the pawnshop. "If you're spending all your time with Brian Frank, who is running the shop?"

"I have employees for that," Eliot smiled.

A loud car horn blared on the street in front of us. I looked up to see Duncan parked in the slot next to my car and eying me impatiently. "We have to go," he yelled.

"Who is that?"

"The office tool."

"Why is he here?"

"That's a really good question."

I walked to the side of Duncan's car. "What are you doing here?"

"Making sure that you make it to the press conference on time," Duncan said dismissively.

"I know how to do my job," I countered.

"Not everyone thinks that," Duncan scoffed.

Eliot moved to my side and regarded Duncan with a serious expression. "Can I help you?"

"Who are you?" Duncan asked.

"Eliot Kane."

"The private investigator working for Brian Frank?" Duncan looked incredulous. "You're interviewing him without me present? I'm telling Fish."

"I wasn't interviewing him," I argued.

"Then what were you doing?"

Eliot slid me a sly glance. I pretended I didn't notice. "That's none of your business. How did you even know I was here?"

"I saw your car. It's not like anyone else has *Star Wars* stickers on their car."

"I'll be over at the sheriff's department in a few minutes. Why don't you go on without me?" I prodded.

"What are you going to do?"

"I'm going to get a coffee and then head over there," I blew out a sigh.

"This is the idiot with the camera," Eliot said suddenly. "The one with the camera strapped to his head at the candlelight vigil."

"I'll have you know that's a state-of-the-art piece of equipment," Duncan shot back.

"You got it at Radio Shack for $100," I pointed out.

"When I win an award for this video, you won't think it's so funny."

"I'll always think it's funny."

"Is this the guy that filmed you fighting with the Channel 7 reporter?" Eliot asked.

Speaking of that. "By the way, Duncan, if that's still up on YouTube when I get back to the office this afternoon I'm going to tell everyone that your wife left you for a Central American drug lord."

It was common knowledge in the office that Duncan's wife, a beautiful Hispanic woman, hadn't been living with him for several months. After sending money to her mom in Central America every week for a year, she had went down to visit her mom three months ago – and hadn't returned.

"That is not true!" Duncan practically shrieked.

"And not only did she leave you, but you're spending your time watching gay porn to deal with your abandonment issues," I continued.

"I'm not gay!" No, Duncan isn't gay. He is a rampant homophobe that owns *Brokeback Mountain*, though. Make your own conclusions.

"When I'm done telling the story, you'll be one step away from dancing naked in that homosexual *Cabaret* revival in Ferndale," I threatened.

Duncan jumped out of the car and moved towards me. His face was red with rage. Eliot stepped between us smoothly.

"You clearly have issues," he said to Duncan.

"And she doesn't?"

"I don't care about her issues. If you touch her, though, you won't be touching anything again for a very long time – and that includes yourself when you're watching your gay porn."

Eliot has a funny sense of humor sometimes.

"Are you threatening me?" Duncan was incensed.

"Yes," Eliot said simply.

"I could report you to the police," Duncan whined.

"You could. That will only make me angry, though. And you wouldn't like me when I'm angry."

You've got to love a guy that quotes *The Incredible Hulk*. Well, at least in my world.

Duncan opened his mouth to unload what I'm sure was a ridiculous retort. Instead, he snapped his mouth shut.

"Good boy," Eliot poked him.

I turned to Duncan. "There's no sense of you going to the sheriff's department. Why don't you go out to the neighborhood and see if you can get any of the neighbors to talk on the record?"

That was a fruitless endeavor. The neighbors were agitated with the constant media presence and had started putting signs up on their windows warning the press to stay away. I figured letting them take their angst out on Duncan would be a lot more fun – for me at least – than spending time with him at the sheriff's department.

"Fine," Duncan nodded curtly. I noticed him shoot another venomous glance in Eliot's direction. Like a typical bully, though, Duncan was too scared to actually confront someone like Eliot.

Eliot and I watched as Duncan got back in his car and sped away. "That guy is a total douche."

"He knows. Everyone knows."

"How is he still employed?"

"He's a chronic complainer. Plus, we have a union."

Eliot nodded briefly. "I figured it had to be something like that. The guy has no people skills."

"Most people think he's normal for the first three days, or so. After that, he can't hide that he's a total tool."

"I think that's the problem," Eliot said.

"What is?"

"He's got a really small tool."

I'd often thought that, too.

Twenty-Three

The press conference was nothing short of boring. All of the media was in attendance – again – but the police had no new information to give us. Why were they holding press conferences when they had nothing to report? The only answer was that they were desperate to keep it the lead story in the area news. My guess was, to put pressure on Brian Frank. I couldn't prove that, though.

Shelly kept a wide berth between us for the press conference – which I encouraged. I caught her shooting me dirty looks from across the room a couple of times, though. I resisted the urge to shoot her the finger. I couldn't get in another fight with her – at least not two days in a row.

"You're showing great restraint not going over there and ripping her hair out and feeding it to her."

I turned to see Derrick standing beside me watching Shelly with a critical eye. "I promised Fish I wouldn't get in another fight with her."

"You just don't want to end up on YouTube again."

This was true.

"Do you think your mom has seen it yet?"

Crap, I hadn't even thought of that.

"He's taking it down this afternoon." I was almost 100 percent sure of that.

"How did you manage that?"

"Eliot," I said simply. I didn't bother mentioning the blackmail.

"You got Eliot involved?"

"Eliot just happened to be there when Duncan showed up and picked a fight on Main Street this morning."

"What were you doing on Main Street? Getting coffee?"

"I spent the night at Eliot's."

Derrick looked surprised. "You're doing sleepovers?"

"Don't you do sleepovers with Devon?"

"Yeah. I just didn't realize things were moving so fast between you."

"It's not all that fast. We've known each other for months."

"You didn't decide to date him until a week ago," Derrick pointed out.

"It's been a good week."

"Even though you're still squabbling with Jake's girlfriend."

"I'm not squabbling with Jake's girlfriend," I countered. "I'm squabbling with a pain in the ass television reporter."

"She is a real bitch," Derrick conceded. "I don't see what Jake sees in her."

That made two of us.

"Except that she's really hot."

I cast a disdainful glance in Derrick's direction. "She's not that pretty."

"Compared to Halle Berry, no. Compared to people around here? She's smoking."

"Better looking than Devon?"

Derrick cast a quick glance around to make sure that Devon wasn't within earshot. "Devon is beautiful. Shelly is gorgeous."

I grimaced. I so did not want to hear that. I decided to change the subject. "Why are you guys doing daily press conferences when you have nothing to report?"

"It's easier than answering twenty different phone calls from reporters every day."

"That's not why," I countered. "You're trying to keep this case out there for a reason."

"And why do you think that is?"

"I think you're trying to rattle Brian Frank," I said honestly.

"What if we are?"

"Is it working?"

"I don't know what you're talking about."

Derrick moved away from me and over to the other side of the room where Devon was standing. I hate being lied to. It drives me to the brink of insanity, I swear.

I watched as Jake broke away from Shelly and headed towards me. "Can I talk to you?"

"It's your building. You can do whatever you want."

"Can I talk to you in my office?" Jake's tone was grave.

I followed him soundlessly to his office. I saw that Shelly was giving me a smirk. I had a feeling this conversation wasn't going to have anything to do with the Frank case. She'd better hope I didn't see her in the parking lot when this was over.

Jake ushered me into his office, shutting the door behind us. Through the two open doorways, just before Jake latched the door, I could see Shelly frowning. Obviously she thought she was going to be able to see the showdown.

I turned to Jake expectantly. "What have you uncovered?" he asked. Never what you think.

"Not much," I said honestly. "I know that Sarah Frank was sleeping with her boss. I know he's in the Bahamas, and no one has been able to track him down. I know that you guys are purposely hiding the information about the au pair. I also know you guys are keeping surveillance on Brian Frank."

"Is that all?" Jake was watching me curiously.

"Isn't that enough?"

"I'm just surprised you told me."

"I didn't think it was a big secret," I admitted.

"You know more than the other media does, and yet you haven't printed it. Why?"

"It's all conjecture right now," I said with faux responsibility.

"Or you don't want to tip your hand to the other reporters."

There was that, too.

"Why did you bring me in here Jake? I know you don't want to talk about the case." There it was.

"Shelly told me what happened between you two yesterday."

"Apparently you can see it on YouTube, too."

"I know. Derrick showed it to me when I went to talk to him."

"What do you want me to say?" I looked at Jake helplessly.

"I want you to say that you're going to stop picking fights with Shelly." That was rich.

"I didn't pick the fight. She did."

"She's insecure around you."

"Why?"

"You know why," Jake said evasively.

"How is that my problem?"

"It's not," Jake conceded. "I don't know how to fix this situation, though. I was hoping you would just lay off."

"It's not my job to fix your relationship."

"Of course not. You wouldn't even try to fix our relationship. Why would you try to help me with someone else," he shot back bitterly.

What is that supposed to mean?

"I don't know what you want from me Jake. She picked a fight with me. I'm not going to let her run roughshod over me just because she's sleeping with you. That's not my job. It's not my business."

"Fine," Jake said shortly. I could tell he was angry with me, but I was beyond caring at this point. No, really.

"Anything else?" I raised my eyebrows as I regarded him.

"No, I guess we're done here."

"I guess we are." I turned to walk out of his office, but Jake's voice stilled me.

"Be careful, Avery."

"Of what?"

"Of everything. Things are going to start happening soon."

"How do you know that?"

"I don't know it," Jake countered. "I just feel it."

"Well, thanks for the warning."

"I don't want you to get caught in the middle of this if things take a . . .turn."

"I'll take that under advisement," I said stiffly.

"There's something else," he said.

"What?"

"I'm never going to like you dating Kane," he said.

"I know that."

"He can keep you safe, though," Jake sighed. "If you feel you're getting close to something, take him with you."

The statement surprised me. "I'll be fine, Jake."

"Good," he said. "As much as you drive me crazy, I wouldn't exactly be happy if something happened to you."

"You just don't want to have to tell my mom I'm dead." I was shooting for levity. The sentence came out as hollow, though.

"I don't want you to be dead," Jake said simply. "You make the world more . . . interesting."

"Jake . . . " I started. I had no idea what I was going to say. It didn't matter. Jake turned his back on me.

This whole situation was too much for me to deal with. "Good luck, Jake," I said finally.

"You, too."

"I don't need luck," I scoffed.

"All you have is luck," Jake laughed. He still wasn't looking at me, though. "Luck and an absence of self preservation."

I didn't say goodbye when I left Jake's office. There was nothing left to say. The goodbye was implied – in a lot of different ways.

Twenty-Four

After the press conference at the sheriff's department, I was fairly keyed up. I didn't feel like going to the office – especially since I wasn't sure what angle to take with the story. A third day of nothing new in a row equaled a big old ten inches of nothing in the print product. That wasn't acceptable to me.

I still hadn't heard from Eliot, and I had no idea if he would be able to finagle an interview with the au pair. He was pretty charming when he wanted to be, but if something was going on with the au pair and Brian Frank she was probably trying to keep a low profile.

I decided, instead, to check out Brian Frank's dad's property in Mount Clemens. A cursory search of property records had revealed that his dad owned a machine shop in town – a machine shop that Brian Frank had worked at when he was a teenager. I was hoping some of the workers there would have some insight into Brian Frank's past. In other words, I was hoping they would tell me he was a douche who would have no problem killing his wife. What? That would totally make my life easier at this point.

I drove to the area where the machine shop was supposed to be located. Even though it was close to The Monitor's office, I had never actually been on the street before. It was an industrial area that was full of different car repair shops and smaller manufacturing plants. There were no coffee shops or decent shopping options in sight.

When I parked outside of the machine shop, I double-checked my notes to make sure I had the right address. The place looked totally deserted. Once I was sure I had the right address, I exited my car and looked around. The building was open to the front of the street, but there was a fenced in area along the back. The parking lot, which was only big enough to house about ten cars, was completely empty.

Was this place still in operation?

I walked over to the front door of the facility. It looked dark, but I couldn't be sure it was truly empty. I pulled on the handle, but it was securely locked. I tried to peer in through the glass window at the front of the building, but it was too dark to see anything.

I wandered over to the simple fence on the side of the building. There was no lock on the gate, so I opened it and walked towards the back of the building. Sure, it's technically trespassing, but there were no signs warning people off – so that's a gray area in my book.

As I walked behind the building, I couldn't help but marvel at how grimy it was behind the facility. It's not like I expected a machine shop to be clean – but this was just gross.

The backyard area of the machine shop was pretty desolate. It was completely empty, except for some paint cans propped up by the back door and an industrial dumpster at the back end of the property.

Since the dumpster was closer, I walked to it first. I lifted the plastic lid and looked inside. It was filled with various discarded metal parts and a handful of plastic garbage bags. I picked up the first garbage bag, pulling open the drawstrings so I could glance inside. I wasn't expecting to find anything, so I was surprised when I saw a dirty rag inside of it. The rag was stained with various dark liquids – and one surprising red one. It looked like blood.

I felt my heart start to race a little bit. I tried to calm myself. What were the odds that it was really blood? I figured I was just psyching myself out. It was probably oil or something.

Still, I couldn't stop myself from digging into the bag a little more. I was scared of what I might find, and yet I couldn't stop myself from looking. There was something hard – and sharp – in the bag as well. I couldn't figure out what, though. To get a better angle, I pulled the bag out of the dumpster and dropped it on the ground next to my feet. I glanced around to make sure no one had arrived while I had been distracted, and then dropped to my knees.

I opened the bag wider, pulling out the rag first. The red stains on it had dried and caused the fabric to stiffen. Under the light of day, it looked even more like dried blood. I swallowed hard, dropping the rag on the ground next to me, and then rummaging further into the bag.

The hard item I had felt earlier was a weird plastic handle. It was broken off from something. I reached into the bag again, jerking my hand out when I felt something sharp lodge in my skin. When I looked at my hand, I realized I had a small nick in my index finger.

Instead of shoving my hand back in the bag, I opted to rip the plastic open a little further. I felt my heart tighten when I saw what I had cut my hand on. It was a broken handsaw – and it looked like it was covered in blood.

I stepped back inadvertently and slammed into something hard behind me. I swung around in panic. I was both relieved – and a little nervous – when I saw Eliot standing behind me. He didn't look happy.

"What the hell are you doing here?"

Nope. Not happy to see me.

"I was looking for someone to interview who knew Brian Frank," I said.

"So you searched the garbage?"

"I saw what looked like blood on a rag," my heart was hammering in my chest. "I just wanted to see what else was in the bag."

Eliot took in my chalk white face and shaking hands and pulled me towards him. "Are you alright? What did you find?"

"Look in the bag."

Eliot looked down at the open garbage bag and then turned his searching eyes back to me. "Is it a body?"

"N-n-no," I stuttered. "It's something else."

Eliot looked grim as he released me and knelt to look in the bag. "Shit," he mumbled.

"It's blood, right?"

"It looks like it."

"What are we going to do?" I was shifting nervously.

"We call the police."

That sounded like a really bad idea. "How about we just tip them off anonymously?"

Eliot shot me a dirty look. "No. We're not going to do that. We're going to call them and tell them what we found."

"Jake is going to be really mad," I said.

"No, Jake is going to be pissed beyond belief."

I bit my lower lip. "I'll call Derrick," I said finally.

"You don't think he'll be pissed?"

"No, but his first inclination won't be to lock me up."

Eliot regarded me with his warm eyes. "Jake won't lock you up either. He is, however, going to scream and yell like a banshee."

I blew out a sigh, pulled my cell phone from my pocket, noticing that I had ignored five texts from my mom, and dialed Derrick's cell phone. He had Caller ID, so he recognized my number. "I'm not giving you any dirt."

"Hello to you, too."

"Hello. I'm not giving you any dirt."

"I . . . I found something at the Frank machine shop."

Derrick was silent on the other end of the phone for a minute. "What did you find?" He asked finally.

"A bloody rag and a broken handsaw with blood on it."

"Where did you find it?"

"The dumpster behind the building."

"What were you doing behind the building?"

"Trying to find someone to interview."

"In the dumpster?"

"No. I just looked through the dumpster on a whim."

Derrick sounded like he was trying really hard not to explode on the other end of the phone. "Are you alone?"

"Eliot is with me."

"Was he with you when you went on your dumpster dive?"

"No."

Derrick sighed heavily. "Stay where you are. We'll come to you in unmarked cars. We'll be there in a few minutes."

"Okay."

"Don't tell anyone else about this," he warned me.

"I won't," I promised.

"I mean it."

"I said I won't."

I wasn't sure if Derrick had hung up or not, but then I heard him grumbling on the other end of the phone. "Jake is going to kill you."

Twenty-Five

Waiting for Derrick and the rest of the sheriff's investigators to arrive was pure torture. I was seriously considering getting into my car and bolting. Eliot could deal with the police while I hid under the bed at my house for the next month.

"Don't you even think about running," Eliot warned me.

"I wasn't," I lied.

Eliot didn't look like he believed me. I didn't blame him. I was too keyed up to even attempt a good lie.

Derrick was the first person to arrive on scene. Eliot pointed to the bag on the ground wordlessly.

Derrick looked in it briefly and then turned in my direction. "I'm assuming your fingerprints are all over this."

"Probably," I admitted. "I didn't really expect to find anything."

"You're either the luckiest person I know or the unluckiest," he grumbled.

I was leaning towards unluckiest right now. "Is it blood?"

"It looks like it," Derrick said. "I can't be 100 percent sure. I don't know what else it could be, though."

"What about oil? It is a machine shop."

"Oil isn't red."

"Maybe it's paint?" I said hopefully.

Derrick shook his head. "Even if it turns out to be something besides blood, you're going to be in a whole heap of trouble with Jake."

"Did you tell him?"

"I did," Derrick said morosely. "As much as I wanted him to tear you a new one, I was afraid he would freak out in front of a bunch of people and try to throttle you. Then Eliot would step in and everyone would go to jail."

"What did he say?"

"He started swearing like a sailor and hung up. I'm fairly certain he'll be here when he calms down a little bit. You may have handed us a big break here, after all."

"I don't think he's going to see it that way," I countered.

"Probably not."

We lapsed into silence for a minute. I felt my phone vibrate in my pocket another two times. Since it was probably just my mother freaking out because I'd ignored her earlier texts, I decided to keep the streak alive and really unhinge her. I didn't think I could keep my fingers from shaking long enough to type on the phone anyway. "Where is everyone else?" I finally asked.

"The tech team had to get their equipment. They'll be here in a minute."

"Why didn't you guys search this place before?"

Eliot cleared his throat. "Do you really think that's important right now?"

"I was just asking."

Derrick glared in my direction. "We had no reason to search here," he said. "We can't just break into a place and look around. We need warrants and evidence."

"I didn't break in," I argued. "I just walked through the gate."

Thankfully for all of us, the tech team had arrived on scene and was now making their way into the open yard. Eliot led me to the wall of the building. I noticed he positioned me between him and Derrick. I figured it was a strategic move.

The three of us watched the tech guys work in silence for about fifteen minutes. Then I heard a loud voice from around the corner and knew that things were about to get ugly.

"Where is she?"

Derrick exchanged a quick glance with me and then pushed himself away from the building to position himself between Jake and me. "Here it comes."

Jake rounded the corner. His gaze fell on me almost immediately. "You are unbelievable!"

I remained mute. There was no point irritating him anymore than he already was.

"You don't have anything to say to me?"

"Not really."

"If I'm not mistaken, we just had this conversation less than an hour ago."

"What conversation?"

"The one where I told you not to put yourself in a situation like this!" Jake's voice was shrill, and he was gesturing wildly.

"No, you said if I was going to do anything I should take Eliot with me. Look, Eliot is here." I didn't mention the fact that he was only here out of sheer coincidence. Wait, why had he come here? Now probably wasn't the time to ask him that question, I figured.

"You only hear what you want to hear, like always," Jake was ranting now. "It's unbelievable. You just don't listen. It's like you're deaf and dumb."

I opened my mouth to argue, but Eliot shot a hand out to stop me. "Don't," he warned.

"I tell you what not to do and then you go and do just that," Jake was on a roll now. "You ignore the law. You ignore that little voice inside of you that tells you that what you're doing is a stupid idea. You ignore your family. You ignore me." He glanced in Eliot's direction. "I bet you don't listen to him either."

I knew he was nowhere near being done, so I just sat back and waited for him to get everything out. I didn't really have a leg to stand on in this argument anyway. I needed to plot my next move.

"I don't know what chemical imbalance you're suffering from that makes you just walk into these situations," Jake raved some more. "Now you've created a whole mess of my investigation."

"Actually, I think I helped you." I don't know why I open my mouth sometimes. Seriously.

"You helped me?" Jake's eyebrows were practically melding with his hairline.

"Garbage pickup in the city is tomorrow. If I hadn't looked in the dumpster, no one would have found this."

Jake took a step towards me. His face was so red I was momentarily worried that he was going to have a heart attack right in front of me.

Eliot stepped in front of me protectively. I knew it wasn't necessary. Even as irate as he was, Jake would never actually physically hurt me. "She knows she made a mistake," Eliot said calmly. "Screaming at her isn't going to change anything."

"No, but it will make me feel better," Jake grumbled.

The tech officers were still working dutifully, but I noticed they were occasionally shifting their eyes up in Jake's direction occasionally. They seemed nervous.

Jake was now pacing a five-foot path in front of us. He was muttering to himself, but I could still hear every fifth word or so. Moron and idiot seemed to be his favorite options at this point.

I turned to Eliot dubiously. "I told you we should have just made an anonymous call."

Jake stopped pacing and rounded on me in disbelief. "You weren't going to call us?"

"I wonder why?" I said sarcastically.

"Yeah, this is all my fault." Jake started pacing again.

After about an hour, the tech guys finished up and were carrying the bag of garbage to the front of the building. A second team of tech guys were now searching through the rest of the dumpster.

Eliot and I followed Jake and Derrick, who were trailing behind the first set of tech guys, back to the front of the building. Jake hadn't said anything else to me since his last explosion, but I did notice him shooting me angry looks on occasion.

When we rounded to the front of the building I stopped in disbelief. All four area news vans were parked in front of the facility. Crap.

Jake looked as surprised as I felt. "What the hell?"

"They showed up a few minutes after you got here," one of his deputies said from the other side of the gate.

"Why didn't you tell me?"

"I was told that would probably be bad – especially given the mood you were in."

Jake glared at me again. "How can this possibly be my fault?" I asked him. "They obviously got the tip from someone in your department. I certainly didn't tell them."

Jake mulled that over for a second. "They probably heard it on the scanner," he said finally.

I noticed that Shelly was moving away from her news van and towards us. She slowed her pace when she saw me with Jake.

I smiled at her with false brightness. "Hi Shelly," I greeted her with faux enthusiasm. "Fancy seeing you here."

Shelly ignored me. "Sheriff Farrell, is it true that you found a body?" She shoved a microphone in Jake's face.

"No, it is not true," Jake argued. "We did not find a body."

Shelly looked disappointed. "What did you find?"

"We're just doing some simple tests for our investigation," Jake said stiffly. "Trying to leave no stone unturned."

Shelly shot a glance at me. I was suddenly interested in the cut on my finger. "What is she doing here?"

"Ms. Shaw was just . . . helping us with our investigation," Jake gritted out.

I raised my eyebrows in surprise. "I was?"

"You were," Jake confirmed. "Her help has been invaluable." I could tell that statement hurt.

"How did she help?" The venomous tone of Shelly's voice was pretty frightening.

When the other news representatives caught sight of Jake, they all rushed around us and started shoving their own microphones in Jake's face. "Did you just say that Avery Shaw is helping you with the investigation?" The question had come from Devon – and she didn't look any happier than Shelly was.

"I did," Jake said. "I cannot go into details right now. Our investigation, including Ms. Shaw's part in it, is not open for public consumption."

Shelly looked dumbfounded. "So she gets to know what's going on and we don't?"

Jake grimaced. "I guess you could say that. Although Ms. Shaw will not be printing anything from the investigation in her publication at this point."

I hadn't agreed to that. I opened my mouth to argue my point but Eliot wasn't taking any chances. He clamped his hand over my mouth to make sure I couldn't say anything stupid.

"She doesn't look like she's agreed to that," Shelly pointed out. "Personally, Sheriff Farrell, I don't think it's particularly fair that Ms. Shaw is getting better information than the rest of us."

"Oh, that's rich," Devon shot back. "Since you've been getting special treatment from the sheriff yourself, I don't really think you have any place to complain."

"I have not been getting special treatment," Shelly argued. "He hasn't told me anything, no matter how hard I try. He says he can't talk about an ongoing investigation."

I couldn't help but wonder exactly how hard she had tried – and what her methods of interrogation had involved. My guess was a thong and love cuffs.

"Besides," Shelly continued. "You're not exactly innocent in this. You're sleeping with one of the deputies involved in the case."

I glanced over at Derrick. His cheeks were reddening under the sudden scrutiny of the media throng.

"Don't equate my relationship with Derrick to your social climbing with the sheriff," Devon challenged Shelly. "What Derrick and I have is real. What you have is ruthless ambition."

I was starting to like Devon.

"Everyone knows he's always going to favor Avery over you, anyway," Devon charged on. "He can't help himself. No one can figure out why. She's nuts."

The love is gone.

I turned to Eliot. "We should probably go."

"I couldn't agree more."

Eliot and I slunk away, leaving Jake to deal with his media harlots and me to wonder how I was going to explain this to Fish. So much for getting off his shit list.

Twenty-Six

Eliot and I said our goodbyes on the street. When I had asked him why he was at the machine shop, he had been evasive and didn't answer the question. I figured that he was going to do exactly what I had done – he just didn't want to admit it.

When he left to get in his truck, I couldn't help but notice that he didn't give me a kiss goodbye – or ask me over to his place for the night. He must be really mad.

I went back to the office, dreading the lecture I was about to get from Fish. I had no choice, though. I needed some direction on where I should take my investigation next. I didn't think that Jake's orders were enough to stop us from printing what I had found, but I wasn't sure if that was the way Fish would want to play it. We really couldn't afford to piss Jake off at this point.

Fish was waiting for me when I entered the building. "You did it again," he said.

"What?"

"You got personally involved in a story."

"It's not my fault. I went to the machine shop to try and find someone that has known Brian Frank for a long time. It just happened."

Fish shook his head distractedly. "I don't know how you do it?"

"Just lucky, I guess." I was going for cute. I think Fish read it as deranged.

"What did you find?"

I figured Fish had met me in the reception area because he didn't want to risk anyone else hearing what I had stumbled on. After I told him, he seemed to consider our options in silence for a few minutes. "We're not going to run anything tonight," he said finally.

"Are you sure?"

"The sheriff clearly doesn't want anyone to know what we've found," Fish said. "He's not going to tell anyone else. If we run with this, we run the risk of getting something wrong. We'll wait."

I was silently relieved. I didn't want to piss Jake off anymore than I already had. "So what do we tell everyone?"

"Nothing."

"Nothing? You know that's not going to work. They're going to be on me the minute I walk into the newsroom."

"Then don't go in the newsroom," Fish said simply. "Go to a coffee shop and email me a short story that just covers the press conference. Then you can be done for the day."

"You're rewarding me with an afternoon off?" I couldn't help it, I was surprised.

"I don't see a lot of other choices, do you?"

"Not really," I admitted.

I followed Fish's orders and went to a coffee shop downtown. It only took me about twenty minutes to write up the story and ship it off to Fish. I was now at a loss what to do with the rest of my afternoon and evening.

When my cell phone started to ring, I felt a jolt of anxiety course through me. I could only hope it wasn't Jake – or my mom. I didn't want to talk to either of them right now. I was relieved when I saw Carly's number pop up.

"Hey."

"The wedding is off!"

This was about the tenth time the wedding had been called off due to a Carly freak out in the past six months. I wasn't particularly worried that this one would hold. "What's wrong now?"

"His mom wants me to sign a prenup," Carly choked out.

"Why? It's not like Kyle owns anything of value?"

"She says that I'm a gold digger and I'm after her family money."

"Does Kyle's family have money?" I knew his mom drove a Bentley, but I figured that was just because she was pretentious.

"They're have some money. It's not like they're rich, though," Carly replied.

Carly was a well paid accountant for an insurance agency. I wasn't quite sure what Kyle did – but I didn't think he earned a lot of money hawking whatever Internet wares he was peddling on a regular basis. "So? Sign it. You'll make more money than him anyway."

"That's not the point," Carly sounded irritated with me now. "She's already planning for our divorce."

"You've called off the wedding ten times," I pointed out.

"Don't be a pain"

"I'm just saying, from her perspective, you might seem a little fickle." I'm loyal to Carly, but I'm also honest.

"I didn't call you to be rational," Carly argued.

"Oh, sorry. She's a bitch. You want to egg her car again?"

"No, she would know that was us," Carly pointed out. We had done just that a few months ago. Even though Harriet Profit couldn't prove we had done it, I knew she had her suspicions.

"What do you want to do?"

"I suppose you have to work tonight?"

"Actually, I'm done for the day."

"You want to get drunk?"

That sounded like a great idea – as long as I hid her phone so she couldn't drunk dial Kyle or his mom late in the evening and I hid my own so I couldn't do the same. "Always."

"Come over to my parents' house. They're gone for a long weekend. They said I was a bridezilla and they needed a break from me."

I could see that.

"I'll be over in an hour."

"Bring a fifth of something."

"What? Hot Damn?"

"No. I haven't been able to drink that since we threw up on it that one time."

"Whiskey?"

"Yeah. Bring sour mix, too." That would be much more pleasant to throw up on.

"See you soon."

I arrived at Carly's with a fifth, two packs of smokes, and a handful of DVDs.

"What did you bring?"

"I didn't know what you would be in the mood for, so I grabbed *The Goonies* in case you wanted to laugh, *My Girl* in case you wanted to cry and *The Shining* in case you want to fantasize about killing someone," I explained.

"*The Shining*. Definitely."

That was my choice, too.

Carly started mixing drinks while I popped the movie into the DVD player. She seemed calmer already.

"Have you talked to Kyle today?"

"He says he doesn't want to talk to me if I'm just going to threaten to call off the wedding, again."

"Won't you be glad when you're finally married? Then you can start to threaten him with divorce."

"We're getting married in the Catholic church," Carly said. "We can't get divorced. I'll have to threaten him with an annulment. My mom will pitch a fit if I get divorced."

"Well, that will be just as fun."

Carly turned to me suddenly. "How are things with Eliot?"

I told her about my day, not leaving anything out. I knew Carly wouldn't tell anyone. She was stunned when I finished.

"You've had a shitty day."

"Yeah."

"How long do you think Eliot will be mad?"

I shrugged. I had no idea.

"How long do you think Jake will be mad?"

"Only a year or so. He eventually forgives me. He'll throw it in my face forever, though."

"Well, at least he didn't arrest you," Carly offered helpfully.

There is that.

After watching *The Shining*, we were ridiculously drunk. We decided to take a walk around the block to get some air and sober up. The walk turned into an hour-long affair, especially after Carly fell in her neighbor's bushes and I couldn't anchor myself well enough to pull her out, so I fell in, too.

It took us almost a full five minutes to extricate ourselves from the bushes. When we finally did, I couldn't help but notice a man sitting in a blue SUV parked across the street from us –

about three houses down from Carly's parents' house. It was dark, so I could only make out a silhouette, but the occupant was obviously staring at us.

"Who is that?" Carly asked, slurring her words a little.

"One of your neighbors," I don't know.

"It's probably Mr. Peterson."

"Does he own a blue SUV?"

"I don't know. It's a big truck like that. He's probably going to tell my parents I was drunk."

"You're an adult, why would they care?"

"Why do you still wear *Star Wars* shoes to specifically drive your mother insane?"

Point taken.

Carly and I carefully made out way back to the sidewalk and headed towards her house. I stopped once to see if the man was still staring at us. He was. I shot him the finger, which Carly quickly tried to cover up.

"Don't do that."

"He's a dick."

"You don't even know him," she admonished.

"Any guy who watches two girls fall in a bush and does nothing to help them is a dick."

"You have a point," Carly ceded, turning around and flipping off Mr. Peterson, too. She would regret that in the morning, I figured.

When we got back to Carly's house, we both passed out on the floor. For such a shitty day, the evening had actually turned out to be somewhat fun. I doubted I would be feeling the same way in the morning, though.

Twenty-Seven

I woke up with one thought on my mind: I think I'm dying.

My head felt like something was pounding at my cranium trying to get out, my mouth was dry and my eyes were practically crusted together. I groaned in pain when I felt the sunlight from the window hit my eyes.

"I'm never drinking again," Carly moaned next to me.

"We always say that. Then we dry out long enough to forget what this feels like and we do it again," I reminded her.

"I blame you."

"How is this my fault?"

"You brought the whiskey."

"You told me to."

"You ignore everyone else in the world when they tell you to do something but you suddenly listen to me?"

"What can I say? I'm easily manipulated."

I climbed to my feet and grabbed two bottles of water from the refrigerator. I handed one of them to Carly, who was rummaging in her purse for a bottle of aspirin. She handed me two, which I swallowed wordlessly.

"What time is it?" I asked finally.

"I don't know," Carly said. "Why? Do you have to work?"

"Yeah."

I dug tin my purse until I found my cell phone. I grimaced when I saw that I had missed six calls – two from Lexie, two from Eliot, one from Derrick and one from a blocked number. None of them had left a voicemail. I had also missed six texts from my mother – all of which had gotten increasingly dire, and threatening. I had also missed one FaceTime request from her – which I was actually thankful for. In my drunken stupor, I would have probably accepted it – and then never heard the end of it. Great.

"What time is it?" Carly was looking at my phone over my shoulder.

"It's a little before eight," I said.

"Looks like you were popular last night?"

"Yeah, that's me, little miss popular."

We both jumped when my phone started ringing. Eliot's number popped up. "Hey," I greeted him hoarsely.

"Where are you?"

"Carly's."

"I was worried about you. You just disappeared and then you didn't go home last night."

"Carly was having a meltdown and I was a little anxious so we decided to approach our problems with a fifth of whiskey and *The Shining*."

"That's a great movie."

"It is," I agreed.

"You still should have called me. I was worried."

"I thought you were mad at me," I admitted.

"I am. That doesn't mean I'm not worried about you, too." Eliot's words were sweet but his tone was gruff.

"That's sweet, but I'm perfectly capable of taking care of myself." I glanced over at Carly, who was pulling shrubbery from her hair. I smothered a bizarre urge to laugh. Carly saw me smiling in her direction and reached over and pulled a twig out of my hair and waved it in front of my face. Okay, maybe it wasn't that funny.

"I didn't say you weren't capable of taking care of yourself," Eliot barked. "You just seem to wander into trouble, though. For all I knew you could have been lying dead in a ditch."

"Nope, just falling down drunk in a bush."

"What?"

There really was no way to explain that. "Have you heard anything else?"

"We're not done talking about you yet," Eliot countered.

"Eliot, I'm an adult. If I want to get drunk with my best friend I'm allowed." He was starting to irritate me. The hangover wasn't helping matters.

"I didn't say you weren't. All I'm asking is a heads up on your whereabouts, especially the night after we discover a bloody rag and broken saw while investigating a missing woman."

"I'm sorry," I apologized, even though I didn't really mean it. "I didn't realize I'd picked up another parent, though."

Carly flashed me a thumbs up. "That's the way to get him to forgive you," she said. "Insult him."

"Is that Carly?" Eliot asked.

"Yeah."

"Tell her to shut up."

"Eliot says hi," I said to her.

She smiled happily. "Tell him I said hi back."

"Carly says hi back."

"You're unbelievable," Eliot grunted.

"I'm sorry Eliot. I didn't really think about it. I thought you were mad and I knew I was fine. Next time I'll text you or something."

"Fine," Eliot muttered.

"Fine."

"So what are you doing today?"

"I have to go to the daily press conference. Then I have family dinner tonight."

"Again? You were just there last week."

"It's a weekly thing," I reminded him.

"A weekly visit to the asylum." Eliot was obviously still cranky.

"Do you want to go with me?"

"Not really."

"Are you sure?"

"I'm sure."

"Okay," I said wanly. "I'll call you after the press conference and tell you how things go."

Eliot was quiet on the other end of the phone. I wondered if I'd accidentally dropped the call. "Eliot?"

"Yeah," he blew out a sigh. "I'll pick you up at your house at 4:30 p.m. for dinner."

"I thought you didn't want to go?" I was surprised.

"I don't want to let you out of my sight even more."

That was kind of sweet.

"Why don't we meet there? I don't know how long I'll be at work."

Eliot didn't seem to like the idea, but he obviously didn't want to make a thing out of it. "Okay," he said finally. "Call me after the press conference anyway."

"You got it," I said with faux brightness.

"Uh, don't talk so loud," Carly ordered, covering her face with a pillow.

"I'm going to start limiting your time with her," Eliot warned, but I could tell he was joking. The storm seemed to have passed – for now. "Unless I'm invited, of course."

"You want to get drunk with us?"

"Carly is hot."

"You're a pervert.

"Derrick told me you two used to make out to get free beers at the bar," Eliot explained.

"When did you talk to Derrick?"

"He called me when you didn't answer your phone last night. He was worried. He figured you were with Carly."

"He wasn't worried," I scoffed. "He just wanted to yell at me because of that whole Devon and Shelly fight."

"Or, he was worried about you and that's the way he expresses himself," Eliot argued.

"Everyone is worried about me," I lamented.

"Everyone is worried you'll do something stupid," Eliot countered. "There's a difference."

He had a point.

Twenty-Eight

I showered and changed at Carly's. I dressed in simple jeans and my new "Looking for love in Alderaan Places" T-shirt. Only a true *Star Wars* geek would get it – and my mom would hate it. She didn't find pseudo incest half as funny as I did.

I left Carly sleeping on her couch. I had no idea if she was going to miss work, but I figured she had her own affairs under control and didn't need another pain-in-the-ass mother figure in her life.

I texted Fish and told him I was going straight to the press conference. He didn't text back – which wasn't unusual – so I assumed he had expected me to do just that.

When I got to the sheriff's department, I wasn't surprised to see Derrick loitering around the main entrance. He clearly wanted to talk to me before I went inside.

"Hey," I greeted him warily. "What's up?"

"I just wanted to make sure you were still alive," Derrick shot back snarkily.

"Please, I already know you're phone buddies with Eliot," I scoffed. "I'm sure he already texted you and told me where I was. Actually, I bet you knew where I was the whole time."

"With Carly? Yeah, I figured that out."

I paused before entering the door – mostly because Derrick wasn't making a move to follow me inside. "What's going on?"

"Why do you think anything is going on?"

"Because you're shadowing me like some creepy lurker."

"I'm just making sure you make it inside the building safely."

"Even I can walk without killing myself."

Derrick regarded me solemnly. He didn't speak, even though his mocha eyes said volumes.

"You're supposed to escort me in and out of the building aren't you? Make sure I don't get in any trouble?"

"I wasn't specifically ordered to do that," Derrick replied. "I was however told that when you arrived, it might be a good idea to keep you in my office until the press conference starts."

"Why? Is Jake on the warpath? Or is it Shelly?"

"I think it's pretty much everyone," Derrick said evenly.

"Great."

"This can't come as a surprise to you?"

"It doesn't," I admitted. "I'm actually surprised I'm being let into the building at all."

"It's a public building."

"Yeah, but Jake . . ."

"Jake is more worried than angry at this point. You've totally fucked things up, but things can always get worse. And, I think he's actually worried that you'll somehow find a way to make them worse."

Well, that was a little insulting.

I followed Derrick into his office, throwing myself into the chair across from his desk. "I didn't know you were phone buddies with Eliot."

"He was worried," Derrick pointed out.

"He was overreacting," I corrected him.

"You cause a lot of people to lose their senses," Derrick smirked.

I bit my tongue to keep the sharp retort on the tip of it from escaping. Derrick was one of my only allies in the department at this time, I couldn't piss him off – anymore than I already had – at this point in time. It would be counterproductive.

I changed the conversation direction instead. "Have you talked to Lexie lately?"

"Yeah, last night when I was looking for you."

"And?"

"And? And she's crazy."

"She's your sister."

"And I can admit she's crazy."

"She's not crazy, especially for our family. She's just a little eccentric."

"She thinks she's going to be able to start a yoga studio?" Derrick looked beyond doubtful.

"She might be good at it."

"Don't you think she should actually teach yoga before she tries to own her own business specializing in it?"

"Yeah, but she doesn't think like you and I do."

"Don't equate my thinking patterns with that tangled mess you have," Derrick grunted.

"I'm just saying we should encourage her. It's good for her to have a dream."

Derrick shrugged. Even he couldn't argue with that. "Did you know she has a boyfriend in rehab?"

"Yeah, Raymond, she told me."

"Is he black?"

"Dominican."

"There's a difference?"

"He's fancy black."

"He's probably just another loser, and I'm not saying that because he's black but because he's in rehab."

"We can't change her taste in men. That's beyond both of us."

Derrick sighed. "I know."

We sat in his office in relative silence for the next fifteen minutes, and then he led me to the conference room. He stopped outside the door before we entered. "I wouldn't ask any questions if I were you. We can't afford the press conference to suddenly become about you."

"Wait, this isn't about you guys arresting Brian Frank? I figured things were essentially over."

"You figured wrong," Derrick countered.

"What? How is that possible?"

"Just go in there, take your notes, and keep your mouth shut," Derrick warned me. "I'm telling you, now is not the time to be . . . well, you."

I entered the conference room and scanned the crowd. All the usual characters were here – including Shelly and Devon. Shelly was busy trying to pretend she hadn't seen me, but Devon was heading in our direction.

"Great," Derrick muttered under his breath. "Do not pick a fight with her."

"I won't." Unless she picks a fight with me first.

"What's going on?" Devon got straight to the point.

"What do you mean?" Derrick asked evasively.

"What were you two talking about?"

"How Lexie wants to open her own yoga studio," I replied. It's technically the truth.

Devon looked surprised. "Didn't she just get out of rehab?"

"Yes."

"Does she even have any money?"

"No."

"Well, that's a stupid idea."

Here's the thing, Derrick and I both thought this was a monumentally stupid idea buried in a mountain of Lexie's other stupid ideas. It's one thing for us to say that to each other, and quite another for someone else to say it. My family closes ranks around their own.

"That's not really for you to say, is it?" Derrick barked.

Devon looked surprised by his tone. "I'm sorry. I didn't mean to . . . I didn't mean to insult her."

Derrick softened his tone. "I'm sorry. We just had a big discussion about this and I don't really want to talk about it anymore. It will just give me a headache."

"Or an ulcer." What? I was trying to be helpful.

"Remember what I said," Derrick warned me, before moving off with Devon. I could hear her questioning him as they stepped away. "What did you tell her?"

I turned my attention to the podium at the center of the room. Jake had arrived when I had been distracted. He didn't make eye contact with me. Actually, he didn't make eye contact with anyone – including Shelly.

The press conference was short and sweet. Jake told the assembled media that nothing had changed. Sarah Frank was still missing. Investigators had no reason to believe that she was dead – although they had no reason to believe she was alive either. In other words, the whole thing was still a mystery.

"But what evidence did you uncover at the machine shop yesterday?" Shelly asked.

"We don't know that we've uncovered anything," Jake said earnestly. Anyone that didn't know him would think he was telling the truth. I knew better. Even if I didn't, though, I would know he was lying. He has a tell, and it's his left eye squinting just slightly. I never told him I knew that, though. I didn't want him to change his behavior. "We're still looking at some things taken from the back of the building, but it doesn't look like they're actually tied to this case."

That was another lie.

I met Derrick's gaze across the crowd. He was gauging my reaction. I wisely kept my mouth shut.

After a few more questions, some of which revolved around me and which Jake swiftly sidestepped, the press conference was over.

"Well that was a waste of time," I heard Devon whisper to Derrick as they moved past me.

"We don't have anything and we can't manufacture evidence," Derrick answered her.

I decided to slip out of the conference room as quietly as possible. I didn't want Jake's attention focused on me. Unfortunately, there are two different doors into the room – which meant two different exits. Jake had used the other one and we ran into each other in the hallway.

"Hey," I greeted him lamely.

"Hey."

"Um, good press conference."

Jake shook his head in disbelief. "Yeah, it was an Oscar-winning performance."

"What do you want me to say, Jake? I already said I was sorry."

"I don't want you to say anything. In fact, the sheer absence of the sound of your voice is the best present you could ever give me."

"There's no reason to be rude."

Jake took a step towards me, causing me to stumble back and hit my head on the cement wall behind me. I inadvertently lifted my hand to the back of my head and rubbed it ruefully. Jake was still invading my personal space.

"I'm not being rude," Jake hissed. "I'm tackling this situation the only way I know how. Now I want a promise from you."

"What?"

"I want you to promise that you're going to stay out of this."

"I promise."

Jake narrowed his eyes as he regarded me. "I mean it."

"I have no interest to get any further involved in this case. Trust me."

"I don't trust you," Jake shot back.

"Then trust the fact that I have family dinner tonight so I can't get involved." I'm always pragmatic.

Jake searched my face for traces I was lying before finally taking a step back. "Maybe you should have family dinner for the whole weekend?" He suggested.

"Yeah, that would drive me crazy."

"It would be a nice change of pace for me, though."

"I told you I wasn't going to get any further involved – and I meant it," I repeated.

Jake moved sideways to allow me to leave. "I'm trusting you, Avery. Don't make me regret it."

I left the building without looking back. I could feel Jake's eyes trained on my back for the entire trek down the hall, though. He obviously didn't trust me. He was right not to.

Twenty-Nine

If I was smart, I would have listened to Jake and returned to the office. I would have filed a mundane story. I would have gossiped with my friend Erin. I would have made fun of Duncan. I would have listened to whatever dating havoc Marvin had wreaked the night before. Then I would have let Eliot drive me to family dinner.

No one has ever called me smart.

Instead, despite my own mind telling me to do just the opposite, I found myself driving out to Romeo. I hadn't been out to the house in days, but I was relieved to find the streets empty – no media presence in sight. They were probably all getting lunch before coming back out here. If the evening news reports were any indication, trucks were parked out here for the 5 p.m. and 10 p.m. news shows every night.

I parked on the street in front of the house, grabbed my notebook and exited my car. Brian Frank had told all of us that he was available for interviews, so I technically wasn't invading his privacy. The fact that I hadn't told anyone where I was going was probably not one of the smarter things I had ever done – but that list was short anyway.

Still, it was broad daylight. I didn't think anything would happen to me in the rich suburbs a full six hours before darkness hit.

I knocked on the door. I was surprised when Brian Frank answered it almost immediately.

"Mr. Frank, I'm Avery Shaw from The Monitor," I introduced myself.

"I remember you," he said. He was staring at me with an emotion I couldn't quite pinpoint. I was leaning towards disdain. He wiped the look off his face just as quickly as he expressed it, though, and plastered a wide smile on instead. "What can I do for you?"

"I wanted to just check-in with you and see how things are going. I haven't seen you in a few days."

"I've done interviews with the television reporters every night."

"I've seen them," I acknowledged.

"What do you think?"

That was a weird question. "What do you mean?"

"How do you think I've been doing?"

"Really good," I lied. "You're a natural at this."

He shrugged sheepishly. "I'm doing the best I can. I just need to find my wife, and I have to stay in the news to do that."

"That's really smart," I smiled at him wanly.

"Yeah, as long as it brings my wife back, it's all worth it."

Brian Frank opened the door and ushered me in. "Why don't you come in?"

I made my decision in an instant, stepping over the threshold and into his garage. I looked around quickly, but nothing seemed out of the ordinary. It was a normal garage. There were two vehicles, one four-door sedan and one blue SUV. The walls were cluttered with various tools, and there was a stack of plastic bins perched by the back door.

"Your garage is cleaner than my house," I joked.

"My wife likes things clean."

"A lot of people do."

Brian Frank led me into this house, motioning towards the dining room table. "Have a seat. Can I get you anything to drink?"

"No thank you. I'm fine."

Brian Frank settled in the chair across from me. "So what do you want to know?'

"Mr. Frank . . . "I started.

"Call me Brian."

"Brian," I corrected myself. "What do you think happened to your wife?"

He exchanged a conspiratorial look with me, his eyes bugging out of his head even more than normal, and then started to talk. "I think she ran off with her boss."

"Dick?"

"Yes."

"Why would you think that?"

"I haven't told anyone this, but they were having an affair."

"You're kidding," I feigned ignorance.

"No."

"How long have you known?"

"A couple of months."

"Have you told the police?"

"No," Brian admitted. "I thought they would think it would give me a motive."

"But you're telling me?"

"You're obviously trustworthy."

Obviously.

"So, why are you telling me now?" I glanced around his house, realizing that it was eerily silent for an abode that housed two small children and an au pair.

"I've read a lot about you," Brian replied. "You're very good at your job. I figured if anyone could uncover the truth about my wife, it would be you."

The look he was giving me was making me extremely uncomfortable, and not just because his eyes were straining in his sockets like a pimple that desperately needed to be popped.

"Where are your kids?"

"At the park with their babysitter," Brian said simply.

"Steffi?"

He looked surprised that I knew her name. "Yes."

"How are they doing?"

"I'm trying to be strong for them. I don't know what to tell them, though. Do I tell them their slut mother ran off with her boss and abandoned us?"

"Probably not," I laughed hollowly. I was starting to feel distinctly uncomfortable.

"No, that's not what a good father would do, is it?"

"No."

"A good father protects his kids. A good father spends time with his kids. A good father doesn't spend weeks away from them."

"You're obviously a good father," I blurted out nervously.

"I am a great father."

I had to get out of here. He wasn't being overtly menacing, but there was something about the aura he was emanating that was making my skin crawl. "I think you're a great father. Everyone I've talked to has said what a great father you are. And what a great husband." Okay, that's a total lie. I needed him to believe it, though.

Whatever was going on in Brian Frank's mind, whatever clouded thoughts he had been mired in, they passed. His eyes lost the hard edge they had only moments before, and he broke out in a wide smile. "People say I'm a great father?"

"Everyone says you're the best father they've ever seen," I lied.

"It's good to see my efforts haven't went unnoticed," he said. "My wife never noticed."

"I'm sure she did," I said lamely. "Some people just don't know how to communicate."

"How are you at communicating?"

I was surprised by the question. "Not great," I admitted.

"I saw you on the news yesterday, you know?"

I swallowed hard. "Yeah?"

"I asked the sheriff, but he said you didn't find anything at my dad's shop."

"We didn't," I lied. "The cops were really there to bust me for trespassing. They just didn't want the rest of the media to know."

Brian Frank visibly relaxed in his chair. "Really?"

"Really."

Thankfully, the silence that had engulfed us was suddenly broken by the sound of the garage door opening and a multitude of feet running into the room. Brian Frank greeted his children with a wide smile and loving hugs, while I fixed my attention on the young woman standing in the doorway.

Eliot had lied when he said she wasn't hot. She had long blonde hair, a heart-shaped face, and wide-set blue eyes. She was also stacked.

I opened my mouth to greet her, but Steffi ignored me and walked into the living room and out of sight. I didn't want to follow her, especially given Brian's unusual behavior. I decided to take advantage of his momentary distraction and excuse myself.

"You don't have to go," he protested.

"I have a story to file and then I have a family dinner tonight," I explained. "I have to be going anyway."

Brian Frank walked with me to the door, patting my back when I paused at the outside door. "Good luck, Ms. Shaw. I'm sure you're going to be important to this story – before everything is said and done."

I turned back to him with a bright smile on my face. "Reporters aren't supposed to be part of the news, Brian. We just report it."

Thirty

I drove to a coffee shop in downtown Romeo and called Fish. I told him I had interviewed Brian Frank, and that I would be emailing my story shortly.

"You shouldn't have gone out there alone," he admonished me. "You should have taken Duncan with you."

"Then he wouldn't have talked to me." Despite the fear I had been feeling inside of the Frank house, I was now calm and mentally chastising myself for my ridiculous behavior.

"You still wouldn't have been alone," Fish pointed out.

"Do you think Duncan would have protected me or helped Brian Frank kill me?"

"I have no idea."

I disconnected from Fish and cranked out my story, waiting until I got confirmation from him that he had received it. Then I called Eliot.

"I'm just going to meet you at the restaurant," I told him.

"Where are you?"

"A coffee shop. I just finished my story." That is not a lie.

"What happened at the press conference?"

"Nothing. Jake said that they were still investigating the evidence at the scene. He wasn't exactly chatty."

"Are you sure you don't want to ride together?" Eliot asked. Since I was so far north, that would be unnecessary and needless travel on my part. I decided not to tell him I was in Romeo, though. I didn't want him to blow a gasket.

"No. I have to stop at the pharmacy anyway. Let's just meet there."

"Okay, but we're not spending the night out there," Eliot countered.

"No one wants that."

"I have a surprise for you."

"Oh, yeah? Is it like a bedroom surprise?" I could really use that about now.

Eliot laughed throatily. "No, but I think I can arrange that, too. It's more like an interview surprise."

Steffi.

"You got the au pair?"

"She's agreed to meet us at a coffee shop in Romeo at 9 p.m. tonight, so we have to keep your family drama to a minimum."

I decided to let that slide. "I'm going to owe you a big thank you," I said flirtatiously.

"I plan on collecting."

During the drive to Oakland County, I ran what I knew through my head. Brian Frank is a weird guy. Sarah Frank was having an affair. Brian Frank knew about it. The au pair might be sleeping with Brian Frank. Dick, Sarah's boss, was still vacationing in the Bahamas — even though the woman he was having an affair with was missing. The whole thing was a giant mess..

When I got to the restaurant, I looked around the parking lot. There was no sign of Eliot's truck. That wasn't surprising, though, since I had been a full half an hour north of him when we talked.

I went into the restaurant and greeted my mom. She raised her eyebrows at my shirt, but didn't say anything about it. "Where is Eliot?"

"He's coming. We drove separately."

She was still staring at my shirt. "What do you think?"

"I think that you have a strange sense of humor, but I've decided not to give you the reaction you want. I'm not going to comment on your clothes anymore."

"Good. Next week I'm wearing my *Shark Week* 'Bite Me' shirt."

"Don't you dare!"

The front door chimed and I looked up expectantly. The smile that was initially on my face disappeared when I saw Derrick and Devon enter the establishment. Shit. I so did not want to see her. Thankfully, Eliot walked in the door right after them.

Eliot slid into the booth next to me, greeting my mom warmly. She was just as happy to see him. Any animosity she had once harbored for his long hair and tattoos had since disappeared. I couldn't decide if that made me happy or not.

Derrick and Devon situated themselves at the middle table. Neither of them acknowledged my presence.

We ordered dinner. I hadn't eaten all day – and I was still slightly hung-over – so ordered my grandpa's special spaghetti. Eliot ordered the same.

After the waitress had left, my mom turned to Derrick and Devon. "How are you guys doing? I keep seeing you on television every night Devon. You're doing a very good job on this Brian Frank story."

What am I? Chopped liver?

"Thank you," Devon said graciously, shooting me a pointed look. "I appreciate you watching my newscasts."

Yeah, we're all thrilled.

"That man obviously killed his wife," my mom continued. "I don't see why Jake just doesn't arrest him." She turned to me curiously. "What did you find in back of that building?"

"I don't know what you're talking about," I lied.

"I saw you on the television," my mom chided me. "The camera does add ten pounds, by the way. I know you were up to something."

Eliot was shaking with silent laughter next to me.

"They busted me for trespassing," I lied. "I didn't find anything."

As much as I would like to crow about what I had uncovered, I knew that Derrick would wrestle me to the ground and make me eat raw eggs before he let that happen.

"Is that true?" My mom asked Derrick dubiously.

"It is," Derrick averted his gaze. He could never lie to my mom. That was something I overcame in my teens.

"Well, they should have thrown you in jail," my mom said.

"Thanks, mom."

"That's the only way you'll learn. You were never one of those kids that would just believe me when I told you the stove was hot. You had to touch it yourself to make sure I was telling you the truth."

"That only happened once," I protested.

"Yes, because you burnt yourself."

"When you play with fire, you get burned," Derrick said.

"Thank you, Mr. Fortune Cookie."

Derrick stuck his tongue out at me.

I turned to Eliot. "Still glad you came?"

"Always. It gives me a whole new insight into why you act the way you do."

"Really?" I raised my eyebrows.

"These people have driven you to the brink of insanity. I'm just trying to keep you from toppling over the edge."

"You're a philosopher now?"

"Maybe I always was."

Since our dinner had arrived, and my stomach was growling loudly, I decided to let Eliot's comment go. He watched me eat about half my plate in three minutes and started laughing. "Didn't you eat today?"

"I didn't feel well this morning," I reminded him. "And then I was busy all afternoon."

"You were sick this morning?" My mom asked.

"Not sick. Just nauseous."

"You're not pregnant are you?" She shot a dark look in Eliot's direction, and the panic in her voice was evident.

"I'm not pregnant," I sighed.

"She was hung-over," Derrick supplied.

If I could choke him with his bacon burger I totally would.

"Hung-over? On a week night?"

"I was with Carly," I answered.

"What? Did she call off the wedding again?"

"Yeah, but just for a half hour or so."

"I don't see why Kyle puts up with her," my mom clucked.

"Probably because she's hot – and she sleeps with him."

"That's as good a reason as any," Derrick agreed.

Devon shot him a dirty look, but my mom's trumped it. "That's not funny, Derrick."

"Sorry," he mumbled.

We all looked up as my grandfather seated himself at the far end of the table. When he saw Eliot, he looked surprised. "You're back?"

"You seem surprised?" Eliot replied.

"You spent a day with us. Most people with any sense run for the hills."

"I think your family is nice," Eliot said simply.

"Give it time," my grandfather said before digging into his own plate of spaghetti.

"This is really good," Eliot said to the table.

"It's a secret family recipe," I teased.

"Can you cook it?"

Like all my cousins, I had spent time working in the restaurant as a teenager. I actually could cook, but more often than not I opted not to. "I can cook," I said cautiously.

"That's going to be my thank you," Eliot decided. "You're going to cook me dinner."

"Thank you for what?" My mom asked suspiciously.

Uh-oh.

I kicked Eliot under the table as a warning. "I have a present for her after dinner tonight," Eliot said evasively.

"What present?"

"Um . . ."

"It's dirty sex mom," I blurted out. Such a mistake.

"Avery Elizabeth Shaw! You do not tell people that in public."

"Then don't ask," I grumbled.

The rest of the dinner was decidedly uncomfortable. Once we were done, Eliot and I said our goodbyes. We didn't speak to each other until we were outside of the restaurant.

"Another fun family night," Eliot laughed.

His phone started to ring at this point; he looked down at the screen and then up to me. "It's Brian Frank."

I waited as he answered the phone. His part of the conversation was brief. When he disconnected, he turned back to me. "He wants me to stop by the house."

"Okay," I said. "I can meet the au pair by myself and then just let myself into your apartment when I'm done. I have a key now.."

"That you do," Eliot said with a laugh. He closed in on me and gave me a long, lingering kiss. "Don't fall asleep," he warned me. "I have plans for you. And be careful with the au pair. I don't think she's involved, but she still might be dangerous."

"I won't fall asleep," I laughed.

I watched as Eliot drove away and then headed towards my own car. I pushed the button to unlock it – even though you didn't need to lock your vehicle this far north – and I heard a crunch on the gravel behind me.

I could only hope it wasn't my mother and she didn't want to talk about my sex life anymore. I squared my shoulders and made to turn around, but whoever it was had maneuvered in behind me.

I felt an arm go up across my mouth and press a cloth there. I could smell the faint traces of medicine. I tried to struggle away, I really did, but I fell into blackness again. My last thought was that this had happened to me before – and only a few months before.

Nothing good ever comes from family dinner.

Thirty-One

I woke up slowly.

It took me a few minutes to get my bearings and realize where I was.

At first, I thought everything had been a dream and I was home asleep in my bed. I don't usually sleep sitting up – or with my hands bound behind me, though – so that fantasy died a quick death.

The next thought that went through my mind was that my eyes had been glued shut. That was an utterly terrifying feeling, until I realized that whatever drug had been used to knock me out was just making the lids feel like they were anchored in granite.

The third thought I had was that I was never going to live this down with my mom – if I lived that long. Of course, Jake and Eliot were going to be massively pissed, too – and I honestly couldn't fathom how they would blame me for this snafu. I knew that they would, though.

I was trying to get a feel for my surroundings, without alerting whomever had taken me that I was now conscious. It only took me about a minute to realize that I was in a car. Michigan roads are some of the worst in the country. Even on a paved road you can't go for more than a couple hundred feet without hitting a pothole that will knock your fillings loose.

I tried to open my eyes just enough to see if we were on a highway, but the window to my right was completely dark. There was no way of knowing where I was.

My next order of business was to figure out exactly who had me. I could feel a figure next to me in the car – but I couldn't make out who it was without actually opening my eyes, and I didn't think that was in my best interests at this point.

The radio was on, and it was turned to some current hits station. There hadn't been a break in the music yet, so I couldn't tell if we were still getting Detroit area stations or not.

The figure next to me had been silent up until this point. "I know you're awake."

I recognized the voice and, truth be told, I wasn't surprised. Brian Frank.

"Why did you take me?" I opened my eyes fully and took my full situation in for the first time.

I was sitting in an upright position, with my hands bound behind my back, in the passenger seat of his blue SUV. Thankfully – or depending on what kind of driver he was unthankfully – I wasn't strapped in to my seat.

"You know why I took you," Brian said, never taking his eyes off the road in front of him. At least he seemed to be a conscientious driver.

"Actually, I'm still not clear on that," I said.

"You knew."

"I knew what?"

"That she's dead."

"I actually didn't know that," I countered.

"Really? Isn't that why you came out to the house today?"

"I just came out to interview you," I lied.

"You really shouldn't treat me like an idiot," Brian said. He was eerily calm. It was actually worse than if he had been screaming and threatening me. It proved he was thinking – and he clearly had a plan in mind. "I'm not an idiot."

"If you knew the cops were closing in, why didn't you just run?"

"What do you think I'm doing now?"

"Most people don't stop and kidnap a newspaper reporter before they run from the cops," I pointed out.

"I'm not most people."

He had a point.

"Where are we going?"

"Away."

"Away where?"

Brian ignored my question. Instead, for the first time since I woke up, he fixed his cold eyes on my face. "What did you find at the machine shop?"

Should I lie? Probably not. It was better that he believe the cops knew everything. "Bloody rags and a saw."

Brian nodded stiffly and then turned his attention back to the road. It was pretty foggy out. That's a regular occurrence this time of year, when the ground is still warm and the nights turn swiftly cold. In the dim glow of his headlights, though, I did manage to catch sight of a highway marker – it showed that we were still on I-75. The upcoming exit marking was for Saginaw. We were heading north.

"Nothing else?"

What else was there? "Not that they told me," I said honestly. "Why? Was her body in there?"

"No, not in the garbage. Part of her was on the roof, though."

Part of her? Eww.

"Why did you put her on the roof?"

"I didn't think anyone would look for her there."

"What p-p-p-part of her?" Even for me, this was a disturbing conversation.

"Her torso. I moved it there from the woods the other day."

"You cut her up and put her in the woods?"

"I didn't know what else to do," Brian said simply.

I swallowed hard. "Tell me what happened, Brian. Maybe I can help." When dealing with crazy people, it's important to make them believe you're on their side. Sure, they're usually paranoid and it doesn't work – but it's better than nothing.

"We were arguing," he started. "She was getting ready to go on another trip with Dick. I knew they were sleeping together. She wasn't having sex with me. She hadn't in a really long time. I told her what I suspected. I expected her to deny it. She laughed at me, though."

I watched him closely for signs that he was about to become unraveled, but he was just as calm as he had been when I first regained consciousness. I had no idea if that was a good or bad sign. I was leaning towards good – for the moment, at least.

"She told me that she had to find a man, a man that had goals and wasn't happy being a house husband. That was pretty ridiculous coming from her, since it was her idea that I stay home and take care of the kids in the first place."

"Sometimes people think they want something until they get it and then they realize it's not how they envisioned," I offered slowly.

"How is that my fault?"

"It's not," I said quickly. "Tell me the rest of the story."

"We were fighting because I told her that I thought she needed to spend more time with the kids," Brian said. I could see the relief actually roiling off him. He just wanted to tell someone what had happened. "I told her she shouldn't go on the trip and stay at home. She told me that she was going with Dick, and when she got back she was filing for divorce.

"Divorce," he said bitterly. "We don't get divorced in my family. Marriage is forever. A promise is forever. She gave up on forever."

I sat silently and let him talk. I didn't think telling him that she probably should never have married him was going to be productive at this point.

"I grabbed her arm when she tried to leave the room," Brian continued. "I just wanted her to listen to what I was saying. She smacked me across the face and told me I wasn't a man, and she needed a man. I just snapped."

"Then what happened?" I prodded him. I wanted to know everything just as much as I didn't want to hear any more of the lurid tale.

"I grabbed her around the throat," he said. "I didn't even really squeeze that hard. I just wanted her to take it back. I wanted her to take those words back. She started panicking when she realized she couldn't breathe and she started clawing at my wrists. I let up for a second. I really didn't want to hurt her."

Brian turned his glassy eyes in my direction. He wanted me to understand that this was all some sort of terrible accident.

"I also realized that I was stuck," he continued, turning back to the road. "She would have me arrested. She would take my kids away. She would take my kids and raise them with that man. I couldn't have that.

"I started squeezing again. I squeezed hard. I couldn't let her take my kids. She was gone in a few seconds, I swear. She didn't suffer."

"Where were your kids?"

"Asleep," Brian said simply.

"Where was Steffi?"

"Asleep."

"No one heard anything?" I couldn't quite believe that.

"We argued all the time," Brian explained. "It was nothing new."

"So, everyone in the house was asleep and your wife was dead on the floor. Why didn't you call the police and tell them it was an accident?"

"The old accidentally strangling your wife defense doesn't seem to go over well in the court system."

He had a point.

"But why did you chop her up?"

"I didn't at first," Brian said. "I just knew I had to get her out of the house before anyone woke up."

He lapsed into silence for a minute, clicking his brights on and off to see if that helped with the dense fog. It didn't.

"A dead body is heavier than you think," Brian said suddenly. "I thought I could just pick her up and move her. She's not very big, you know? She was too heavy, though. Then I thought I could drag her, but it was too hard. I have a bad back.

"I knew I needed some leverage, so I took my belt off and wrapped it around her neck. That way I could pull her down the steps with the belt."

I was suddenly sick to my stomach thanks to the verbal picture he was painting.

"It took me about fifteen minutes to get her down the stairs, even with the belt. I had to stop a couple of times and rest. I was terrified that someone would wake up and come see what I was doing, but no one did.

"When I got her downstairs, I hauled her out to the garage. I managed to get her in one of those plastic storage bins. She just kind of folded up inside. It looked like she was sleeping."

I doubted that.

"I used a piece of wood as a slide and pushed the bin up in the back of my truck and shut the door. Then I went to bed."

"I bet you had nightmares," I said with faux sympathy. I was trying to get him to trust me, even though I was wishing I had my own belt to strangle him with at this point.

"Actually, I slept like a baby."

That's the sign of a true sociopath, I thought.

"So what did you do the next day?"

"I pretended that she went on the trip."

"You just left the body in the car?"

"What was I going to do with it? I had to pretend it was a normal day. I went with Steffi to the park and watched the kids play. We all had dinner. I even read them bedtime stories."

What a great dad.

"Steffi could tell I was upset, so I told her that Sarah and I were breaking up. She didn't seem surprised."

I bet.

"We had a few drinks together and . . ."

"You slept together?"

"We made love," Brian corrected me. "It was the best night of my life, other than the fact that I still had to get rid of Sarah's body. I decided that I wanted to make a life with Steffi. She's a much better mother than Sarah ever was.

"The next morning, I drove my truck to my dad's machine shop," Brian said. "It's been closed for the past few weeks for retooling. I knew no one would be there. So I took her body inside and cut it up.

"It was harder than I thought it would be. The first saw broke. I had to get a bigger saw. When I was done, I wrapped each piece in plastic and put it back in the bin. Then I went home.

"After everyone was asleep, I took her body out into the woods around the park. I couldn't carry the bin out there, so I borrowed my kid's wagon and put the body parts in it and pulled it behind me.

"I spent hours trying to hide each piece. Then, after I was done, I realized that if I left it in the plastic then I was leaving evidence behind. I had to go back and get all the plastic off, but it was almost dawn.

"I went back home and returned the next night. It was hard to remember where I had hid everything, but I managed to find everything and take the plastic off. While I was out there, though, I figured out that her torso was too big to hide.

"I tried to cut it smaller when I was in the machine shop, but it was too hard. You can't cut through bone, you know? I tried to hide her torso in different places. I even found a hollowed out tree log and climbed inside with it. I just didn't feel comfortable leaving it out there. It was too big."

Yeah, that was the problem with this story.

"So I left everything out there and wrapped her torso back up and put it back in the bin. The next day, I went back to the machine shop and hid it on the roof. I figured that even if they searched the machine shop, they wouldn't look on the roof.

"My mistake was throwing everything away there," Brian said. "I didn't realize they weren't picking up the garbage regularly because the shop was shut down. I thought I was already safe until I saw the shop on the news. Until I saw you on the news."

My guess was that he didn't exactly have warm and fuzzy feelings for me. "I'm sorry I ruined things for you." I didn't mean for it to come out as sarcastic as it did, but my nerves were pretty raw at this point.

"Oh, you will be," Brian planted his gaze on my face. The malice in his eyes was clear.

Thirty-Two

"What are you going to do with me?" I really didn't want to know, but it seemed like the question to ask in this situation.

"I haven't quite decided yet," Brian said honestly.

"Why did you even bother to come get me?"

"I don't know. I just figured you were responsible for ruining everything."

"You could have taken Steffi and the kids and ran?"

"Not after you turned her against me."

Uh-oh. He knew Steffi had agreed to meet up with Eliot and me. "She told you she was meeting us?"

"I heard her talking to your little boyfriend."

"Still, you could have taken the kids and ran?"

"That's no life for kids," he said practically. I was surprised he actually realized that. Maybe he wasn't such a bad father – just a bleeding tragic husband.

"Who is with them now? Steffi?"

"No, Steffi is not with them. They're asleep. They're fine."

"You left them alone?" So much for father of the year.

"Your boyfriend will find them."

"That's why you called Eliot? To take care of your kids?"

"I Googled you after you left. I read about your family restaurant. I remembered what you said about dinner. After I heard Steffi on the phone with Eliot, I confronted her. She tried to deny it, of course, but it was too late."

"What did you do to her?"

"I brought her with us."

I looked around the interior of the SUV. It wasn't easy given the way I was bound, but I was fairly certain no one was in the back seat.

"She's in the hatchback," Brian supplied.

"Is . . . is she in a bin?"

"I had never taken it out of the car, so it was easier."

"Is she alive?"

Brian shrugged. "Probably not anymore."

I felt a rush of panic. He had clearly lost it.

"She never should have betrayed me," Brian said.

"You called Eliot from the parking lot of the restaurant?"

"I was hoping to get you alone, but when I saw him with you I knew that I would have to do something to separate the two of you."

"So you didn't really send him to your house to take care of your kids?"

"It's just an added benefit."

I let the ominous silence in the vehicle that followed spread until I wasn't almost completely incapacitated by fear. Then I started to let the anger creep in. This guy was as much of a tool as I originally figured he was.

"Everyone knew from the beginning," I told him. I was done being nice.

"Knew what?"

"That you killed her."

"No they didn't," he protested. "I had everyone fooled. I was a distraught husband looking for the wife that abandoned him."

"You only thought that," I challenged him. "We told you that to your face, but behind your back everyone was saying you did it. The cops thought so, too. That's why they kept having press conferences out at your house and letting you talk to the media whenever you wanted to. They were giving you enough rope to hang yourself with."

"That is not true! You ruined this for me!" Brian wasn't even pretending to be calm anymore. I preferred him in his natural state.

"You didn't fool anyone – except maybe yourself. Why do you think the cops have been keeping such a close eye on you? Why do you think they've let a simple missing persons case completely monopolize the evening news? Think!"

"I did think! I had this all thought out until you ruined it!"

"And what were you going to do when they found her body?"

"They would never even have looked for a body if it wasn't for you," he pointed out.

"Maybe, but you can't be sure of that."

"It doesn't matter now, does it?" Brian said grimly. "It's over for me – and it's over for you."

"So, where are we going?"

"Sarah's family has a cabin up in Traverse City. I figure they won't think to look there for a couple of days at least. We'll be able to spend some time together. Alone."

That sounds fun – or crazy.

We made the rest of the trip –a full two and a half hours – in complete silence. I figured that Eliot had figured out what had happened by now and that he'd called Derrick and Jake. They would have no idea where to look for me, though. I couldn't rely on them. If I was going to get out of this situation, I was going to have to do it myself.

Once we got off the highway, Brian started checking the GPS on his phone. I could only hope they were tracking his GPS – or mine. I tried to shift to feel if my phone was still in my pocket. I felt it buzz with an incoming text – and was momentarily relieved I had set it to silent when my mom's texts started going into stalker territory. Even if they couldn't track Brian's phone, they could track mine – as long as Brian didn't find it.

The roads we were now traveling down were completely dark. There were no street lights in sight. We were really in the country now. I hated the country even when a madman wasn't kidnapping me, so this was essentially my worst nightmare. The only thing that could have made it worse was sharks.

Brian turned down a dirt road at one point, and we were now going pretty slowly. I figured we were close to our destination. When he finally stopped the car, I saw a small cabin – which couldn't have been more than two rooms total – in front of us.

"This is the cabin?"

"Yep."

Brian got out of the car and came over to my side of the vehicle. I considered running, but I knew I wouldn't get very far. He led me to the back of the SUV, opened the hatchback, and grabbed a bag.

My eyes fell on the blue bin, which was tightly sealed. Could Steffi still be alive?

Brian seemed to read my mind. He opened the top of the lid and peered inside. Even under the dim light of the interior of the car I could see she was dead. Her sightless and terrified eyes were fixed directly on me, but she couldn't see me.

"I guess she's dead," Brian shrugged.

"You seem real heartbroken about it."

"Like I said, she shouldn't have betrayed me."

"You're a real prince," I grumbled.

Brian grabbed my arm roughly and led me to the cabin. He unlocked the door and shoved me inside. I couldn't see in the dark and crashed into an end table and then fell on the floor.

Brian flicked the light on, locked the door behind us, and stepped over me. He didn't bother to help me up. He dropped his bag on the floor and immediately turned the small television set on before sitting down on the couch.

I glared at him from my positioned on the floor. Instead of trying to get back on my feet, I rolled to a sitting position and remained on the ground. I didn't want to be any nearer to him than I already was.

Brian flipped through the channels before settling on the local news stations. I wasn't surprised to see the exterior of his house on the screen. We may have been hours away from the scene of the crime, but this was still big news.

I saw Devon come on the screen and explain that police had found Brian Frank's children asleep and alone in the house. They were now in the custody of their aunt – Sarah's sister.

"Great, that bitch has my kids."

"At least they're not alone," I grumbled.

Brian ignored me and turned back to the television where Devon was explaining that police were now searching for Brian Frank and Steffi. There was no mention of me.

"It looks like they don't even know you're gone yet," he crowed.

I doubted that was true. When I didn't show up at Eliot's apartment, he would have started looking for me. I had felt a few more texts silently vibrate in my pocket. I had no idea who they were from, though.

"So what now?"

"Now? Now I'm getting some sleep."

"What about me?"

"Now you're going to shut up."

Not likely.

Brian must have read the intent in my eyes because he pulled a handkerchief out of his bag and gagged me with it, leaving me on the floor. He then switched off the lights, laid down on the couch and proceeded to fall asleep within a few minutes.

Only a complete psycho could fall asleep in a situation like this.

I couldn't get comfortable – and I was trying to focus on the fact that I had to go to the bathroom – so I didn't drift off for hours. Unfortunately, when I finally did fall asleep, I still had no idea how I was going to get out of this situation.

Thirty-Three

The next morning I woke up feeling every muscle of my body cramp in abject pain. At least it was keeping my senses sharp.

Brian was still asleep on the couch, so I took advantage of the situation and tried to wriggle my arms free. My wrists were essentially chafed raw, but I kept at my task. It was my best chance at this point.

To my surprise, I felt the ropes slacken a little bit. I have small wrists, but my hands aren't especially big, so I tried to see if I could pull my hand free. I felt it shift a few inches. If I could just get it to shift a few more inches, I would be free. I kept maneuvering my hands, biting my lip to keep from crying out in pain. I was surprised when my hand popped free.

I looked up at Brian Frank in startled shock. He was still asleep – and I was free.

I tried to get to my feet, but they were numb from the position I had been in over the past few hours. I quietly rubbed them, trying to restore circulation. The pricks in my soles were painful, but I ignored them.

When the pain started to subside, I carefully got to my feet. I almost fell over when I felt the blood rush to all of my extremities, but I managed to keep my footing. I moved towards the door, casting the occasional glance over my shoulder to make sure that Brian was still asleep.

I took a deep breath and flicked the lock. It made a loud "thwack." I swung around to see Brian Frank in a sitting position and staring at me.

"You're not exactly graceful," he said. He hadn't made a move to get to his feet.

"That's not one of my strengths," I acknowledged.

"I saw you and your friend that night in the bushes," he said.

I was surprised. He had been the one sitting in the blue SUV in the dark. The one watching us.

"You flipped me off," he continued.

"I figured you were some demented pervert getting off on two girls rolling around on the ground together," I shot back. "Looks like I was right."

"Where do you think you're going to go?"

"Away from here is fine for right now."

"I can't let you go," he said simply.

"You can't make me stay."

Brian set his mouth grimly. "That's where you're wrong."

I watched with morbid fascination as he pulled a knife out from his bag. It wasn't just any knife either. It was one of those long hunting knives that men use to gut their prey. Nice. I swallowed hard.

"It will be easier if you don't run," Brian said.

"I'm not easy," I said, and then I opened the door and bolted through it. I didn't stop to get a sense of my surroundings. I knew I had to keep ahead of Brian, so I ran headlong into the woods.

I had no idea what direction I was heading. I had no idea where the road was. I had no idea if I was about to topple over a cliff. All I knew was that I couldn't let Brian catch up to me.

I could hear him entering the woods behind me. I didn't figure he was in any better shape than I was – and we were both desperate. Adrenaline is a great equalizer, so I ran.

You might think this is the first time I've ever been in the woods. You would be wrong. When we were kids, Derrick and I spent hours playing *G.I. Joe*. We strategized, plotted and tracked each other through the dense trees. I was pretty good at it.

This wasn't exactly childhood games, but Brian Frank wasn't exactly Cobra Commander either.

As I was running, I felt my phone buzz in my pocket again. My phone! I had forgotten it. I reached into my pocket, slipping behind a tree and out of sight, to look at the screen.

It was a request on FaceTime – from my mom. I didn't hesitate, I clicked the accept button. I was never so happy to see anyone in my entire life.

"Why haven't you called me back?"

"Because I was kidnapped," I snapped back.

"I thought that Derrick made that up," my mom said dismissively.

"Well, he didn't," I said grimly. I scanned the woods behind me for Brian, but I didn't see him.

"You need to tell Derrick that I'm in Traverse City at Sarah Frank's family cabin."

"They're already up there," my mom scoffed. "They tracked your phone."

"Then where are they?"

"Have you looked at yourself? You're filthy."

"I'm hiding in the woods from a guy with a big knife," I pointed out.

"Then maybe you shouldn't be talking on the phone," she chided me.

"You called me," I reminded her.

"I wanted to make sure you were okay," she said finally. "Are you really hiding in the woods?"

"Yes."

"Then why are you getting cell phone reception?"

That was a pretty good question.

"I must be near a highway."

"Maybe you should hang up until Eliot and Jake find you."

"They're both here?"

"That's what Derrick said. He went with them."

The relief that washed over me was immense. It was also momentary. Where were they?

"Who are you talking to?"

I looked up from my crouching position behind the tree and saw Brian staring down at me. He was sweaty and red-faced – and he looked really angry.

"My mom," I said honestly.

"Who are you talking to?" My mom asked irritably.

"Brian Frank."

"Is that really wise?"

"Probably not," I ceded.

"You should probably run," she said pragmatically.

"Probably."

I watched in mute horror as Brian reached down and took my phone from me. He looked at my mom's disgusted face for a moment before throwing the phone against a tree. I watched it shatter helplessly.

I got to my feet and faced Brian resolutely. "They're coming for me," I informed him.

"They won't make it."

"I wouldn't be so sure." I turned when I heard the snap of a twig and about fell over when I saw Eliot standing there. The look on his face was terrifying, although thankfully it wasn't pointed at me. He also looked exhausted. He was wearing the same clothes from the night before. They were disheveled, and his hair was a mess, but he was still the best thing I had ever seen in my life.

Brian reached for me fervently. I stepped back in surprise, falling backwards and tumbling onto the ground.

Eliot moved towards Brian ruthlessly. He was going to kill him. I had no doubt.

"I'll kill her!" He screeched. He was steadily shrinking in the face of Eliot's furious anger.

"If you lay one hand on her, I'll let Eliot crush you with his bare hands."

I looked up to see Jake stepping into the clearing, leveling his gun at Brian. He looked as irate as Eliot – and just as tired.

"How did you find us?" Brian was flummoxed.

"We tracked the GPS on Avery's phone."

"I didn't even know she had a phone." Brian was mostly talking to himself at this point.

Eliot and Jake were both holding their ground. Neither had made a step towards me, but they were poised to spring into action if the situation warranted it.

"It's over, Brian," Eliot said with barely contained rage. "We need to know where Steffi is."

"She's dead in the back of the SUV," I supplied.

Eliot shifted his gaze to me. "Are you alright?"

"Yeah, but I really have to pee."

Jake shook his head, but he seemed relieved despite everything. "Where is Sarah?"

Brian didn't seem to hear Jake. He was completely lost in his own world.

"He cut her up and put parts of her body in the woods and parts on top of the machine shop."

"On top of it?" Jake looked confused.

"On the roof."

Eliot's face was a mask of unexpressed rage at this point. "So you killed two women, left your kids alone at home and decided to take my girlfriend on a camping trip?"

Jake grimaced at the word "girlfriend" but he didn't make a move to interrupt Eliot.

"Why don't you tell me why I shouldn't just kill you right here?" Eliot asked. He wasn't joking.

Brian looked panicked. "You can't let him kill me?" He begged Jake.

"I could say I never found you," Jake suggested. "That Eliot killed you in self defense to save Avery."

"You wouldn't do that," Brian looked flabbergasted.

"No," Jake said grimly. "As much as I would like to, I wouldn't do that."

Brian dropped the knife and took a step towards Jake with his hands outstretched in front of him. Jake pulled his handcuffs out and snapped them on, never moving his gaze from Brian Frank's distressed face. "Why did you do this?" Finding reason with a madman is fruitless, I thought.

Brian looked nonplussed. "It was an accident."

Eliot moved to help me stand up, pulling me into his arms briefly. Once I was steady on my feet, he pulled away and inspected me for injuries. I was still staring at Brian Frank's back. I couldn't figure out how such a small man held so much evil.

Jake looked over at me. "Are you sure you're alright?"

"Is he going to prison forever?"

"Yes."

"Then I'm great," I said before promptly bursting into tears.

Jake and Eliot looked shocked – and then pained. They both just stood there looking at me with dumbfounded confusion.

"Jesus Christ," Derrick walked into the clearly and directly over towards me. "She's a girl. She cries."

"I've never seen her do it before," Eliot said.

"I haven't seen it since we were kids," Jake informed everyone.

"Well, now you have seen it. Stop staring at her."

Derrick wrapped an arm around my shoulders and led me out of the clearing. Jake led Brian Frank a few paces behind and Eliot brought up the rear. "Maybe you should try not to be such a hard ass," Derrick suggested. "You just scared them more by crying than you did by getting kidnapped."

I wiped the tears from eyes and barked out a hollow laugh. "I really do derange people. You were right."

"You can't help it. You were born that way. That's why you're never boring."

I heard Eliot and Jake laugh as we walked out of the woods.

Thirty-Four

When I woke up the next morning, I bolted straight awake with a sense of terror. Eliot wrapped me in his arms quickly and pulled me back down to the mattress with him. "You're okay," he murmured into my hair.

The events of the previous day came rushing back to me. After Jake had taken Brian into custody, he had been transferred back down to Macomb County. Derrick had did the honors. The police wanted to question him over the ride.

After getting my statement, Jake had released me to Eliot's care. Once I stopped crying Jake and Eliot had returned to normal. Both of them verbally lambasted me for going out to interview Brian Frank alone the afternoon before – but, in the grand scheme of things, it could have been a lot worse than it was.

Jake talked to his deputies back in the city and found out they had discovered Sarah Frank's torso on top of his dad's building. Search parties were being organized to find the rest of her in the woods.

Jake had called my mom to tell her everything was fine. She was more concerned with Brian hanging up on her than anything else. She was glad the "rude young man" had been taken into custody. Of course, she didn't know that he had killed the au pair or cut his wife up into little pieces either. I couldn't wait for that conversation. Thankfully my cell phone was dead – so I wouldn't have to worry about that for awhile.

I had fallen asleep in Eliot's car on the way back home. I slept for almost four hours straight. When we got back to town, he took me straight to his place. I climbed into the shower – and I wasn't exactly surprised when he joined me. Instead of a fun time, though, he spent the entire time gently washing me – paying special attention to the miasma of bruises that were steadily popping up. Given the grim set of his mouth, I couldn't help but figure that if he had it to do over again, he would have snapped Brian's neck right there.

We both tumbled into bed after that – not even bothering to get into pajamas. I fell asleep with Eliot's body wrapped protectively around mine. We were both too spent to do anything else.

"How do you feel?" Eliot asked.

"Sore," I admitted.

"I bet."

I groaned as I moved to get out of bed. "I'm hungry," I announced. I had been too tired to eat anything the day before. The last meal I had was grandpa's famous spaghetti.

"You want me to cook for you?" Eliot looked at me suggestively.

"I want breakfast from the Coney."

"That stuff will kill you," Eliot informed me.

"I was already almost killed by a crazy guy, I think I can survive breakfast."

"Fine," Eliot sighed. "Just let me shower."

"Shower later. I need food now."

Eliot shook his head but did as he was told. I would have to take advantage of this situation while I still could. It probably wouldn't last long.

I didn't even bother to put any makeup on. I brushed my hair back into a pony tail, slipped into my dirty jeans and one of Eliot's T-shirts, and headed for the door.

"You're not even going to put on a bra?" Eliot looked amused, and a little turned on.

I turned back to him with a small smile. "You can benefit from that after breakfast."

Eliot didn't put up any argument. Once we got out to the street, he linked his hand with mine for the two-block walk to the diner. I ordered my usual eggs, hash browns, toast and ham and topped it off with some tomato juice. Eliot must have been hungrier than I realized, because he ordered a full breakfast of pancakes and bacon as well.

"That stuff will kill you," I teased him.

"Dating you has already shortened my lifespan," he retorted. "I think I can survive the breakfast."

While we waited, I gave Eliot all the gory details from the previous day. He hadn't asked me a thing during the ride home. He must have realized I needed time to process. While I was telling him the story, his face got continuously darker. "That guy is an animal."

"He's not our problem now," I reminded him.

"We're both going to have to testify at his trial," he reminded me.

Shit. I hadn't thought of that. Fish was going to be pissed. Crap. It hadn't even occurred to me that someone else would have had to cover the story in my absence. I looked around the restaurant and caught sight of a copy of The Monitor. I got up, grabbed the paper, and sat back down. I was relieved to see Marvin's name in the byline spot.

I skimmed the article. He had all of the details. I was a little disappointed that I hadn't gotten the big story, but since I was part of the story that wasn't exactly a surprise.

Eliot watched me read the paper knowingly. "You'll still have the big story. You'll be able to write everything up from your point of view. No one else will have that."

"I know," I said defensively.

"Eat your breakfast," Eliot ordered. "We're going back to bed when you're done."

We both looked up at the front door when it chimed. I was surprised to see Jake walk in. When he caught sight of us, he headed in our direction. He slipped into the booth next to me, reached over and grabbed a slice of bacon off of Eliot's plate, and then turned to me. "How are you feeling?"

"Good," I said. "A little sore, but good."

"Did you sleep?" He cast a wary glance in Eliot's direction.

"For like twelve hours."

"That's good, you probably needed it," he said.

"So what's up?" Eliot asked.

"Brian confessed everything. He's being taken out to the woods to show the deputies where the rest of Sarah's body is this afternoon."

"That's a cheery task," I muttered.

Jake reached inside of his pocket and pulled out a piece of paper, slipping it towards me. I was surprised when I saw it was a check for $25,000. "What's this for?"

"It's the reward from Crime Stoppers," Jake said.

"Reward?"

"For solving the Sarah Frank case."

"I forgot there even was a reward," I admitted.

"That's what happens when you get kidnapped."

"I shouldn't get this," I said. I was suddenly embarrassed. "Give it to his kids or something."

"You solved the case," Jake pointed out. "Put it in the bank."

I looked up at Eliot curiously. "What do you think?"

Eliot sipped his coffee a second and then smiled. "I think you earned it."

Jake sneaked another slice of bacon from Eliot and then got to his feet. "By the way, can you tell your mom to stop texting me and requesting calls on FaceTime?"

"No."

"It's becoming annoying."

"Better you than me."

Jake shook his head and walked out of the restaurant. He didn't look back.

Instead of going back to Eliot's apartment, I returned home. I promised him that not only would I spend the night with him tonight – but I would cook him dinner. I had something I needed to do first, though.

When I got home, Lexie was waiting impatiently for me in the dining room. "I can't believe you didn't call me," she said angrily. "If I wasn't heavily meditating, I would have freaked out."

"Did you say meditating or medicating?"

"Don't be cute."

I told Lexie the gritty details of my travails – she only interrupted me about ten times for clarification – and then I pushed the check towards her decisively.

"What's this?"

"I figured you could start your yoga studio."

"You're giving this to me?"

"No," I cautioned her. "I'm a silent investor in your yoga place. If it goes belly-up, so be it. If it makes a profit, you have to pay me back."

"It will make a profit," Lexie promised.

"I know."

Faith starts somewhere. If the Brian Frank situation had taught me anything, you can't just kill someone else's dream. You have to be willing to support them. I was taking a chance on Lexie. Who knows? Maybe she'll surprise me and be a huge success.

Of course, this could be the world's biggest money trap, too.

Thirty-Five

When I returned to work on Monday, I expected a big lecture from Fish. My bruises were steadily on the mend, but I figured the ego bashing I would get from my increasingly disgruntled boss would be tremendous.

He surprised me when he greeted me with a stiff hug instead.

"I'm glad he didn't kill you."

That's it? "You're not mad?"

"You didn't plan it did you?"

"No."

"Then I'm not mad at you."

There had to be a catch here. "You do, however, have to do a series of articles chronicling your time with Brian Frank. Enough for an entire week."

"That's a lot of articles," I said carefully.

"You'll figure it out."

Great.

My friend Erin watched the exchange with a mixture of worry and relief. "I'm so glad you're alright."

"That makes two of us."

"Was it scary?"

"It had its moments."

Now that I was two days removed from the situation, I was a lot braver in hindsight than I had been in the present.

"Still, you're like a hero now," she enthused, her dark eyes sparkling.

"I don't know about that."

"No, you are," she said honestly. "Everyone loves you."

"Duncan?"

"Well," she amended. "Duncan hates you. Actually, he hates you even more than normal."

"Why? Because I didn't die?" That would be so like him.

Erin bit her lower lip. "I think you better ask him."

"Where is she?" I heard Duncan bellowing from across the room as he entered, leaving a swath of fleeing reporters in his path.

"I assume you mean me?" I fixed my steady gaze on him.

"I can't believe you," Duncan ranted. "You did this on purpose. You completely stole my thunder."

"I stole your thunder?"

"You purposely cut me out of the story because you knew I would overshadow you."

"If you mean that I purposely got kidnapped so you couldn't be a part of the takedown, well, you got me. It was all part of my diabolical plan."

"I knew it," Duncan raved. "I'm going to human resources – and this time there's going to be no way they can keep you. You have officially done it this time."

"You do that," I challenged. "Do you think they're going to fire the woman they've budgeted an entire week of front page stories from?"

Duncan looked properly chastised – for a minute. "This isn't over."

"It's never over."

I walked over to my desk, pulling my new cell phone out of my pocket as I went. Eliot had surprised me with it yesterday. His number was pre-programmed into it – and it was number one on speed dial. Even better, I had forgotten to text my mom to tell her I had a new phone.

I hit his number and waited for him to pick up.

"What's up? Are you okay?"

"I'm fine," I said.

"Just making sure," he mumbled.

"Can't I just call to chat?"

"Not that I've noticed."

"Well, I actually am calling for a reason."

"I knew it," Eliot blew out a sigh. "What have you done?"

I pushed back the angry retort that had bubbled to the surface. I was turning over a new leaf, after all. "Actually, I called to invite you to Carly and Kyle's wedding in a few weeks."

"You called to invite me to a wedding that's almost a month away?" Eliot seemed surprised.

"I did."

"Why?"

"Why not?"

"It's just not like you."

"If you don't want to go, just tell me," I grumbled irritably.

"I didn't say that," Eliot said hurriedly. "I guess I'm just surprised."

"So, do you want to go?"

"It would be my honor."

"You might not say that when you see my dress."

"I guess I'll just have to picture what's under the dress," Eliot said suggestively.

"My Yoda thong?"

Eliot laughed despite himself. "I'll see you later tonight."

"Yes, you will," I agreed.

I disconnected the phone and sat down at my desk to start writing. I had a lot of stories I was expected to produce over the next week. I might as well get a jump on them. The new and improved Avery was taking direct and purposeful action.

I heard a nasal voice waft down the aisle. "She purposely cut me out of the story and you're not going to do anything about it?"

"Oh, shut the hell up!" I exploded.

So much for turning over a new leaf.

Author's Note

I want to thank everyone who takes the time to read my novels.

If you liked the book, please take a few minutes and leave a review. I understand that my characters aren't for everyone. These are not bright and shiny people – and they swear a lot.

This is a work of fiction. Names, characters, businesses, places, events and incidents are either the products of the author's imagination or used in a fictitious manner. Any resemblance to actual persons, living or dead, or actual events is purely coincidental.

All rights reserved. No part of this book may be reproduced or transmitted in any form or by any means, electronic or mechanical, including photocopying, recording or by any information storage and retrieval system, without written permission from the author, except for the inclusion of brief quotations in a review.

Made in the USA
Lexington, KY
09 April 2013